RAGE

RAGE

JOHN MAVIN

thistledown press

©John Mavin, 2017
All rights reserved
No part of this publication may be reproduced or transmitted in any form or by any means, graphic, electronic or mechanical, including photocopying, recording, or any information storage and retrieval system, without permission in writing from the publisher or a licence from The Canadian Copyright Licensing Agency (Access Copyright). For an Access Copyright licence, visit www.accesscopyright.ca or call toll free to 1-800-893-5777.

Thistledown Press Ltd.
410 2nd Avenue North
Saskatoon, Saskatchewan, S7K 2C3
www.thistledownpress.com

Library and Archives Canada Cataloguing in Publication
Mavin, John
[Short stories. Selections]
Rage / John Mavin.
Short stories.
Issued in print and electronic formats.
ISBN 978-1-77187-141-9 (softcover).—ISBN 978-1-77187-142-6 (HTML).—ISBN 978-1-77187-143-3 (PDF)
I. Title.
PS8626.A88465A6 2017   C813'.6   C2017-905313-2
C2017-905314-0

The following stories have been previously published in slightly different forms: "And Apparently, Cigarettes" in *Chameleon*; "Deposition" in *Grain, The Journal of Eclectic Writing*; "The High Alpinist's Survival Guide" in *Prairie Fire*; "Waiting for the Defibrillator to Charge" in *Pilot Pocket Book*; and, an excerpt from "Axel and the *Terrorflieger*" in *Wreck*.

Cover and book design by Jackie Forrie
Printed and bound in Canada

Thistledown Press gratefully acknowledges the financial assistance of the Canada Council for the Arts, the Saskatchewan Arts Board, and the Government of Canada for its publishing program.

Acknowledgements

Hemingway is often quoted as saying "the first draft of anything is shit." While I'm indebted to many people who helped get these stories into a shareworthy form, there are several whom I'd like to publicly thank for their exceedingly generous support: Alison Acheson; Sylvia Bourgeois; Angela Violini Ford; Steven Galloway; Bruce Howe; Elizabeth Mason; Maureen Medved; Paul Millward; Rob Philipp; Jan Redford; Harriet Richards; Laisha Rosnau; Erin Vandenberg; Pablo Vignon Pina; Bryan Wade; Sonia Zagwyn; the wonderful people at Thistledown Press; my children, Katherine and Richard; and most especially, my wife, Jacqueline — the most supportive person in my world.

Thank you.

CONTENTS

9   *Axel and the* Terrorflieger

19   *And Apparently, Cigarettes*

34   *Deposition*

50   *Relevance*

83   *Mercy Manor*

94   *Dal Segno al Fine*

110 *Waiting for the Defibrillator to Charge*

119 *Rage*

177 *The Edmore Snyders*

200 *A Flock of Crows is Called a Murder*

232 *The High Alpinist's Survival Guide*

For Jacqueline

Axel and the *Terrorflieger*

About an hour before dawn on Sunday, March 26, 1944, a teenage German *Obergefreiter* led a handcuffed Canadian airman through the deserted central train station in Frankfurt am Main. Pigeons fluttered between soot-stained Nazi banners and the fraying ropes that hung from the iron girders. Spilled oil, lingering exhaust, and damp smoke from the devastated Römerberg drifted on the chill air. Three-quarters of the overhead windows had been blown out. When they arrived at Platform 24 — the short track near the north wall — the airman sat on a wooden bench and began to smile.

The *Obergefreiter* paused to check his pocket watch. His faded greatcoat, which bore the two chevrons marking his junior rank, was threadbare and much too big for him. His re-issued *Schiffchen* — perched atop his icy-blond hair at an over-earnest angle — was too small. A wooden whistle hung from his neck and he carried a *Kars* — a bolt-action Karabiner 98k rifle — over his right shoulder. He, too, was smiling.

The airman twisted awkwardly to work a creased photograph from his back pocket with his bound hands. Eight days of stubble darkened his cheeks. All he wore was a sleeveless undershirt, grease-stained uniform pants, and a new pair of flight boots. Gooseflesh pimpled his bruised skin. He stank something awful.

The *Obergefreiter* repocketed his watch and motioned for the airman to stand. "*Aufstehen, Herr* Thane."

Rather than comply, the airman bent to look at his photograph. It showed his seven-year-old daughter squinting into the sun in front of his neighbour's rosebush, wearing a floral sundress his wife had ordered from the catalogue.

"Stand up."

"You speak English?" The airman struggled to push his photograph back into his pocket.

The *Obergefreiter* rolled his eyes. "*Herr* Thane, I escort enemy officers to their trains."

Thane got to his feet. "When is the train to Stalag Luft III coming?" When he saw his chin was level with the peak of the *Obergefreiter's Schiffchen,* he asked "what are you, fifteen? Sixteen?"

The *Obergefreiter* put his finger to his lips.

"Answer me, boy." Thane squared his shoulders. "I'm an officer."

The *Obergefreiter* looked beyond Thane to a triple set of doors marked *Nordausgang* and his smile faded. New padlocks secured all three doorways.

"You hear of the Geneva Convention?" Thane unkinked his neck. "You got to show me respect."

"You are a pilot."

"I flew a Halifax. Crew of seven, all looking to me."

The *Obergefreiter* glared and approached the *Nordausgang.* "*Frau* Seiler?"

Axel and the Terrorflieger

"Your interrogators processed those enlisted boys straight away. Assigned them hard labour in a coal mine."

Quickened footsteps echoed from a corridor labelled *Nachteingang* back by Platform 13. A girl in her early twenties emerged, her hair — uncovered and uncombed — was icy-blonde. *"Axel!"* The girl's whisper carried across the empty platform hall. She wore a faded housedress beneath an unbuttoned coat.

"Wait here." The *Obergefreiter* jogged to the girl, meeting her between Platforms 19 and 20. "Erma, *wo ist Frau* Seiler?"

The girl grinned. *"Sie kommt."* Dark circles hung beneath her eyes.

Thane advanced on their position, his footfalls echoing loudly. "She your one and only?" He marched over to Platform 23. "She ever seen a Canadian officer before?"

The *Obergefreiter* ignored Thane as he pointed to the *Nachteingang*. *"Wir brauchen das Seil."*

"Are you saying you shot me down yourself?" Thane crossed Platform 22. Pigeons unsettled in the girders above.

The girl looked into the *Obergefreiter's* eyes. *"Was sagt er?"*

Thane cleared his throat. "You're *Luftwaffe,* right? German air force?"

The *Obergefreiter* turned to Thane and put his finger to his lips again.

"How come you're just a guard?"

The *Obergefreiter* frowned. "Be quiet."

The girl pouted and stamped her foot. "Axel, *erklär mir."* She'd used butcher's twine for shoelaces.

"You fail flight training or something?"

Axel rolled his eyes and turned back to the girl. "*Er kommt aus Kanada.*"

"That's right, I'm Canadian." Thane added some jaunt to his step. "When does this train come to take me to the special officer camp?"

Axel held up his palm.

"My bet is it'll be late." Thane strutted across Platform 20.

"Stop, *Herr* Thane."

"One-Fifteen Squadron blew up your marshalling yard two weeks ago. We were going to hit it again but that night fighter —"

"Halt!"

" — got Turner, right in his . . . turret. I was the last to bail out before the Halifax crashed into this farm house." Thane's voice caught. "I think the family was still inside."

Axel's eyes hardened. "*Terrorflieger!*" He unslung his *Kars* and bashed Thane in the stomach. Thane fell and Axel raised his buttstock over his head.

Thane couldn't help but cower. "Please, no!"

"*Axel!*" The girl gasped, her voice still a whisper. "*Noch nicht.*"

Before Axel could hit him again, a second set of hurrying footsteps sounded from the *Nachteingang*. Axel lowered his *Kars*.

The girl turned as a woman entered the platform hall at a run. "*Mamma!*"

"*Ich komme*, Erma." The woman had knotted a black scarf over her greying hair and had buttoned a black wool coat neatly over her dress. She wore heavy workman's gloves and carried a large canvas bag in her arms. Despite her reduced civilian rations, she appeared strong.

Erma pointed at Thane. "Axel *hat den Terrorflieger.*"

Axel returned his *Kars* to his shoulder. "On your feet." His smile returned.

The woman's eyes were cold and her jaw hard. Taut muscles corded in her neck. "Axel, *bring ihn hier.*" The woman strode directly to Platform 24, her brisk passage relocating the pigeons to Platform 10. "*Schnell, bevor mehr Soldaten kommen.*"

"*Jawohl, Frau* Seiler." Axel pushed Thane forward.

Thane looked over his shoulder as he marched. "Where'd you learn English?"

"You only learn one language in your Canadian school?"

Thane looked away.

When they arrived back at Platform 24, they stopped beneath an empty span of iron girder, three paces from the bench.

Frau Seiler sneered as she unfastened the straps on her canvas bag. "*Er hat Oliver getötet.*"

Thane turned to Axel. "You'll have to translate."

Erma took a deep breath then stepped up to touch Thane's stubbly cheek. "*Sie haben mein Baby getötet.*"

"What's your girl saying?"

Axel rolled his eyes a third time. "Erma is my sister, *Dummkopf.*"

Erma traced Thane's eyebrows.

His eyes widened. "Are you stuck on me?" Thane tried to force a smile. "Because I'm an officer?"

Erma ran her fingers along his jaw line. "*Sie haben mein Baby getötet.*"

Thane gulped. "You want a baby?"

"*Ich töte dich.*" Erma cupped his chin then stood on her toes to press her lips to Thane's.

Frau Seiler circled behind. As Thane closed his eyes and let himself be kissed, *Frau* Seiler withdrew a rope from her canvas bag — one end tied in a noose — and handed it to Axel.

He looped it over the empty girder.

Erma slid her hands behind Thane's ears and gently caressed them.

Thane stifled a sob and opened his eyes. "I can't do this." He tried to disengage.

Erma kept her lips pressed into the kiss.

He spoke into her mouth. "I have a daughter."

"*Tu es!*" *Frau* Seiler shouted, the noose ready in her hands.

Erma twisted Thane's ears and forced his head back as *Frau* Seiler slipped the noose over his outstretched neck.

"What the hell?"

Erma slapped his cheek, hard. "*Er hat Oliver getötet!*"

Before the sting could bloom, Axel took up the rope's slack. "Frankfurt was bombed the night you were captured, *Herr* Thane."

Thane's cuffed hands flailed uselessly behind him. "I wish they'd done a better job."

Erma slapped him again. "*Sie haben mein Baby getötet!*"

Thane looked to Axel. "Why does she keep saying that?"

Axel rolled his eyes again. "My sister does not want to fuck you, you stupid *Arschgesicht*. She is telling you her son is dead!"

"What?"

"*Sterbe!*" *Frau* Seiler twined the rope around her waist.

"Our apartment was near the Römer. Your bombs killed little Oliver in his crib."

Frau Seiler spat. *"Terrorflieger!"*

Axel smiled. "No Stalag Luft III for you." Together, the three Germans winched Thane off the ground.

His face swelled as his throat constricted. "Turner should have crashed . . . into your house."

Tears spilled down Erma's cheeks. *"Mein Oliver."*

Thane's legs kicked spasmodically. Veins distended and burst in his forehead.

Axel tugged harder on the rope. His *Schiffchen* fell to the ground.

Thane rose higher. "My only mission . . . FUBAR."

Axel paled. "What did you say?"

Thane twisted a full circle.

"You are not a pilot."

Thane's voice choked to a harsh whisper. "Mechanic."

Axel swore and released the rope, although *Frau* Seiler and Erma managed to keep Thane suspended. "You told the interrogator you were an officer."

Erma furrowed her eyebrows. "Axel, *was machst du?*"

"Officers . . . don't . . . work."

"Dummkopf." Axel frowned "What is your rank?"

Thane said nothing.

Axel punched him in the chest. "Answer me!"

Thane's eyes bulged. "Aircraftman . . . Second . . . Class."

Axel shook his head. "Allied aircrew are sergeants at the minimum."

"Turner . . . needed . . . gunner . . . got . . . volunteered." Thane went limp.

"*Scheiße.*" Axel bit his lip and turned to the others. "*Lasst ihn los.*"

Frau Seiler pulled harder. "*Nein!*"

"*Er hat niemanden getötet.*" Axel shook his head. "*Wir können's nicht tun.*"

Erma gasped and stepped away from the rope.

Frau Seiler tugged even harder, winching Thane ever higher, his only movement an irregular twitch in his cuffed hands.

Axel raised his whistle and ordered *Frau* Seiler to let go of the rope. "*Soldaten werden kommen.*"

"*Er ist der Terrorflieger!*"

Axel took a deep breath and blew his whistle, loud and shrill.

"*Bitte, Mamma.*" Erma grabbed both of her hands. "*Frau* Seiler!"

"*Er muss sterben!*" *Frau* Seiler elbowed Erma hard in the chest, dropping her to the ground.

"*Er hat uns nicht geschädigt!*" Axel readied his *Kars* and chambered a round. "*Zurück!*"

"*Er hat das Baby getötet! Meinen Enkel!*"

Axel raised his *Kars*.

"*Meinen* Günter!"

Axel shook his head. "*Er hat* Günter *nicht getötet.*"

Frau Seiler withered a glare at Axel.

"*Wenn Sie nicht gehorchen, schiesse ich!*"

Frau Seiler kept tugging.

"*Tu es!*"

"*Nein!*"

Axel grimaced, released the safety, and fired overhead. Shattered glass rained down.

Frau Seiler screamed, letting go of the rope to cover her face with her heavy gloves.

Thane fell to the concrete platform, his face purple.

Erma rushed to his side and untied the noose. "*Bitte verzeih mir.*"

Thane gulped in air and writhed on the ground.

Frau Seiler unwound the rope from her waist then stepped forward to grab Erma's shoulder. "*Dein Ehemann.*"

Erma wiped tears from her face and backed away. "*Günters Kompaniechef schickte diesen Kondolenzbrief.*" She withdrew a folded letter from her pocket and held it up.

Axel lowered his *Kars*. "*Er wurde bei Estland getötet.*"

Frau Seiler snatched the letter.

Axel pointed at Thane, whose colour was returning to normal. "*Er ist unschuldig.*"

A tear ran down *Frau* Seiler's cheek. "*Er ist der Terrorflieger.*"

"*Nein.*" Axel shook his head. "*Er hat niemanden getötet.*"

Frau Seiler brought the letter close to her chest. "*Meinen* Günter." She turned to Erma. "*Ihr* Oliver."

Erma let her tears fall but shook her head, too. "*Nein.*"

Thane began to retch.

"*Feiglinge!*" *Frau* Seiler crushed the letter into her coat pocket then spat three times — once at Thane, once at Axel, and once at Erma.

Erma bent to wipe Thane's mouth. "*Frau* Seiler, *nach Hause gehen.*"

Axel aimed his *Kars* at *Frau* Seiler's chest. "*Jetzt!*"

Frau Seiler spat again, then spun and marched out the *Nachteingang* alone.

After the sound of her footsteps had faded, Axel reslung his *Kars*, and with Erma's help, got Thane cleaned up and onto the bench.

Thane's throat was raw. "Why save me? I'm a nobody."

Axel reclaimed his *Schiffchen* from the ground where it had fallen. "It would be best if you said nothing until you get to Stalag Luft III." He checked his pocket watch then pulled Erma close for a hug as the sound of running jackboots echoed from the *Nachteingang*. "Your train will be here soon."

And Apparently, Cigarettes

Ever since I was a little girl, Dad's warned me to never piss off Mom. So, when I come home late from school suffering from an acute nic fit to find him smoking and drinking a beer on the front steps, my knees start to twitch. He knows he's not supposed to do that. I make a point of looking at the empty driveway. "Mom giving a reading?" I hold out my hand.

Dad gives me the cigarette, smiles, and closes his eyes. "Don't spoil the moment, Katie." Giant maple trees shade Peck Street from the sweltering September sun while the neighbourhood boys play road hockey with a tennis ball. The still air smells like yeast from the new ethanol plant mixed with Dad's sweat. Right now he's wearing one of his pit-stained concert jerseys, cut-off shorts, and work boots over bare feet. "Detention again?"

I take a drag and sit next to him, exhaling slowly to savour the calm washing over me. "Hey, I'm on your side, remember?" Like Dad and drinking, Mom says I'm not allowed to smoke — not because I'm too young, but because she's had a vision. Dad secretly complains how she can't even pick a winning lottery number so he totally agrees her juvenile nonsmoking ban is completely unfair, especially since she smokes a pack and a half every day. However, even though I'm now in grade ten and have double-pierced ears, and he's a grown man in his thirties, we're both too chickenshit to cross her.

Dad opens his eyes. "What'd you do this time?"

"Nothing."

"You going to share that? It's my last one."

I hand him back the cigarette. "I've been having a nic fit all day."

"Where are yours?"

"Martin confiscated them. Smoking on school property."

"That's the third time in two weeks." Dad takes a drag and returns the cigarette. "Come on, Katie, the rules aren't going to change."

"You're not going to tell Mom, are you?"

"Hey, I'm on your side, remember?"

I hold out my hand again. "Can I have a drink?"

"Nice try." Dad watches the hockey game for a bit. After the tennis ball gets stuck under the station wagon on cinder blocks, he turns to me. "Twenty bucks enough for you to spend the next few hours at the mall? Get a burger and a pack of smokes."

I hand him back the cigarette. "It's a school night." Antagonizing Mom for only twenty dollars is just stupid.

"How about forty?"

"Where'd you get forty bucks?"

"Are you going to help me or not?" Dad takes out his wallet and gives me two twenties.

I stuff them in my back pocket. "When can I come home?"

Dad takes the last drag and pushes the spent butt into the bottle. "Eight o'clock?"

"You smooth things over with Mom for me?"

"I promise," he says as Mom chugs around the corner in our rusted-out shitbox.

My knees twitch again. "You better get rid of that." I point at his bottle.

The hockey boys clear the street.

Dad picks up the bottle then slips into the house.

Mom pulls into the driveway.

I unwrap a stick of gum from my pocket and stuff it in my mouth. I test my breath on my palm and chew fast.

Mom climbs out of the shitbox and slams the door. She's wearing her red power suit with the shoulder pads and has twisted her black hair into a bun. "I thought I saw your father."

"Nope, just me." I point at the hockey boys. "Watching the game."

"Of course you are. Did you finish your homework?"

"Um... yeah. All done."

She reaches for the front door.

I've got to give Dad time to hide that bottle. "Mom?"

"What is it?"

"Um..."

"Katie?"

"Ah..."

"For God's sake, spit it out."

Not being able to think of a better distraction, I ask about her work. "Did you have any good visions today?"

Mom raises an eyebrow and cocks her head to one side. "Since when do you care about my spiritual readings?"

"Did Mrs. Weathers want you to find her son-in-law again?"

"That's none of your business. The only visions of mine that should concern you — "

"I know. Dad shouldn't drink outside the house."

"And?"

"I should never smoke."

"Because?"

"Because something bad will happen if we do."

I guess I rolled my eyes because Mom turns away from me. "My visions are not a joke."

"But you never say what the something bad is."

"You sound like your father."

"It's just . . . "

She looks me in the eye. "What?"

"Nothing."

"No, you were going to say something."

"It would be nice if you could see something good for a change."

"You know my psychic abilities don't work that way. I can't choose what I see."

I lower my voice. "If you even see anything at all."

"What was that?"

Before I have time to answer, Dad opens the screen door. He's still wearing his cut-offs, but has gotten rid of his boots and is now wearing his good black T-shirt. "Hello, Erica."

Mom takes a deep breath. "Were you drinking on the front step again?"

Dad shakes his head. "Not me." I amazed at how well he lies to her. He's so brave. "Was I Katie?"

"Nope." I concentrate on my gum.

Mom points at something on the top step. It's a blue bottle cap, ringed with condensation. Her voice chills. "Then what's this, Tim?"

Mom takes another deep breath so I've got to say something quick. "That's mine. I mean it's my fault," I say. My knees twitch again. "I got Dad a beer but he didn't want it. He put it back in the fridge and told me to wait and give it to him later. Inside. After dinner. When you said it was okay. Before."

Mom hands Dad the bottle cap. "You promised."

I share a look with Dad. "I'm going to the mall, okay?"

Mom blows past us and slams the door. "Both of you, inside."

"But Dad said . . . "

"Now."

Dad holds the door for me.

I whisper a quick "sorry" and follow him to the kitchen where homemade macaroni and cheese waits on the table. A red rose lies on Mom's plate. The table's set for two. Dad tosses the bottle cap in the garbage then gets me a plate and a fork.

"You want the forty bucks back?"

Dad shakes his head. "Don't worry about it."

Mom marches into the kitchen and throws her purse on the counter between the ashtray and the phone. She's taken off her suit jacket. Damp tendrils of hair curl around her ears. Patches of sweat stain the front of her blouse. "Let me guess, Katie made dinner while you weren't drinking out front."

"Dad made it." It's his speciality, macaroni and cheese with cut-up hotdogs.

"We both made it," Dad puts his hand on my shoulder.

I smile. "Do you like the flower?"

Mom smells the rose. "Where'd you find the time? A full day at work, dinner on the table, a long-stemmed rose, and a beer on the step where everyone can see you."

Dad keeps his tone light. "I got off early." He opens the fridge and gets two cans of Coke — one for Mom and one for me — and another beer for himself.

Mom sits at the head of the table. "Katie should have milk."

Dad sets my Coke on the counter. "Sure." He smiles and gets a glass.

Mom scoops macaroni onto her plate. "This is cold."

I put my gum on the side of my plate and take a bite of macaroni. Dad covers everything with breadcrumbs before he bakes it to make it crunch. It's cold and a little starchy. "I like it," I say.

Mom sips her drink and glares at me. I decide to keep my mouth shut.

Dad gives me my milk.

Mom slides her plate forward. "I can't eat this."

Dad sits. "I thought you'd be home half-an-hour ago."

Mom looks ready to bite his head off, so I speak up. "I told Dad I'd keep it warm in the oven, but I forgot."

"I told you this morning I'd be home at five."

Dad takes a deep breath. "Please, Erica, I'm making an effort here."

"You make a dinner I can't eat and I'm supposed to forgive you?" I keep my eyes on my plate. She isn't talking about Dad's beer today.

"I'm sorry." Dad lowers his head. "I forgot you needed the car."

"I'm not just some line worker at the ethanol plant, Tim. I have responsibilities. Even though I'm the only professional psychic in Dolsens, I can't cancel readings at the last minute if I want to grow my business."

Dad puts his face in his hands. "I said I was sorry."

"You agreed to never drink outside the house again." Mom jabs her finger at him. "Ever."

My knees twitch when I realize she's back to talking about today. Sometimes it's hard to keep up.

Dad wipes his eyes. "I've had a bad day."

"You've been saying that for two years." Mom slams her palm flat on the table. The plates jump. "You don't even bother to come up with new excuses anymore."

Dad's eyes are rimmed red. "Please, not in front of Katie again."

I put on my best I'm-being-good-but-this-might-traumatize-me look.

Mom snorts. "You two always cover for each other."

"No we don't," I say.

Mom glares again. "Shut up, Katie. I'll deal with you later."

"Hey, back off." Dad drinks some beer. "You could scar her emotionally."

Mom pushes her chair back. "Stop being so goddamn melodramatic."

"It's not healthy for Katie to see her parents fight."

"Healthy?" Mom launches herself at the counter. She holds up my Coke. "This is not healthy." She throws the can into the sink where it splits open and foams down the drain. "Shit." Mom empties the can then takes it to the garbage.

Dad bites his lip. "Erica, I'll get that."

"What the hell are these?" Mom reaches into the garbage and pulls out four beer bottles, one after the other. She sets them on the counter. They're all beaded with condensation.

I don't even look at Dad. "Mom, I put them in there. I forgot they go — "

"Stop lying to me, Katie." Mom takes her cigarettes from her purse along with her lighter — a pink see-through plastic one. My knees twitch, twice this time. I want a cigarette. No, I need a cigarette. A whole one, just to myself.

Dad finally speaks up. "You think you're so perfect do you, Ms. Independent Business Woman? What are you doing right now?"

Mom looks at her cigarettes and lighter, then at me. She throws them back in her purse, tightens her lips, and sits down.

Dad senses a rare advantage. "You bust my ass for the Coke but you were going to smoke while she eats." The twitch in my knees comes back and doesn't stop.

"Shut up."

"Don't like the truth?"

Mom throws the rose at him. "I said shut up, Tim."

Dad ducks and the flower tumbles across the linoleum behind him. A petal falls off.

I put my hands on my knees to make them stop but it doesn't work.

Mom throws her fork too. "You made me cancel two readings last night while you were at the McCrae House. That's a hundred dollars." We're back to last night's argument.

And Apparently, Cigarettes

Dad jumps out of his chair. "Money? Is that what you want?" He pulls out his wallet. He counts five twenties and throws them at her. The bills land between our plates.

"Where'd you get this? Payday isn't until tomorrow."

"I got it early, okay?"

Mom doesn't touch the money. Instead, she gets up and goes back to her purse. "You can't get it early. You're in a union. Are you playing poker again?"

"Leave the cigarettes where they are."

Mom opens her purse. "If you're going to drink, and Katie's going to lie, then I'm going to smoke."

My knees are going nuts. I want a cigarette so bad.

Dad grabs for her, but Mom pushes him, knocking him into the counter. He slips and falls to the floor.

Mom lights a cigarette and stuffs the pack in her purse. She inhales slowly. "Where'd you get the money?"

Dad just sits there, looking at the floor. I take in as much second-hand smoke as I can. It's not very comforting.

"Answer me!"

A tear slides down Dad's cheek.

"Where?"

Dad swallows twice before he speaks. "I got fired today."

Mom takes a deep drag. "My vision."

Dad nods.

She crushes her cigarette into the ashtray. Smoke curls from the bent tip. Just one little drag. I wouldn't even wipe off the lipstick. Mom twists the cigarette until the smoke dies. "Do you know how hard it is to lose a union job?"

"I've had — "

"Goddamn it, you're useless." She looks at the cluster of beer bottles and picks one up. "You're never going to listen to me, are you?" Mom throws the bottle in the sink. It breaks and brown glass explodes over the counter.

"I've had a bad day."

Mom looks to the ceiling and takes a deep breath. "I told you what would happen."

Dad looks up. "You can't mean that."

She puts her hands on her hips. "Get out."

I can't keep quiet. "Please, Mom — "

She turns on me. "Shut your goddamned lying little mouth!"

I shut up and try to be as small as possible.

Dad starts to stand. "Don't yell at — "

Mom kicks him in the leg and he falls back down. "You're not even eligible for unemployment!"

Dad curls his legs in front of him. "I have nowhere to go."

Mom grabs the hundred dollars from the table. "Sleep at the McCrae. Live in the park. I don't give a fuck. Just get out." She throws the money and it flutters to the linoleum, helicoptering like maple keys.

I can't just sit here quietly. "Mom!"

"I told you to shut up!" She raises her hand to hit me.

Dad points at her. "Don't you dare! Katie comes with me."

Mom takes a deep breath and lowers her hand. "Not a chance."

"I'm not leaving without her."

Mom kicks Dad again.

He falls again.

"Mom, no!" I get up.

And Apparently, Cigarettes

"Sit down!" Mom's skin turns red and blotchy.

I sit.

Dad finally makes it to his feet. "Give me another chance. I promise, I'll stop." He sways.

"You're still drunk." Mom snorts and picks up the phone. "I'm calling the cops."

"Erica."

"9-1-1." She presses a button.

Dad takes a step toward her. "At least I don't hit Katie."

Mom presses a second button. "My daughter is not going to turn into an alcoholic."

"I've never given her beer."

"You don't share it with anyone!"

Dad looks at the phone, me, and finally the beer bottles on the counter. He starts to say something but stops. He starts again and this time says, "I need help."

Mom's finger hovers over the last digit. "If you don't move, I'm pressing the last number."

Dad takes the hundred dollars from the floor. "You're breaking up this family."

"This is not my fault."

Dad kisses my forehead and puts the money in my hands. "Come with me."

I look at Mom and my knees shake even harder. "I can't." I lower my eyes.

"Then I guess I'm on my own." Dad leaves the kitchen. The front door opens and slams shut.

Mom hangs up the phone and takes three deep breaths. When that doesn't calm her, she throws the rest of the beer bottles in the sink. "I've been helping him for over fifteen years." Mom looks for something else to throw. Her chest is heaving. Her eyes are wild.

I realize I've made the wrong decision. My knees are jittering so bad I can barely stand. I put my hands on the table and push myself up.

"Where are you going?"

I stuff the money in my pocket. "With Dad."

"No fucking way." Mom crosses her arms and blocks my path.

I will my knees not to give out. "I'm not staying here with you."

Mom takes three more deep breaths. She reaches for her purse again. "Yes, you are."

"He was asking for help and you were a complete bitch."

"Watch your mouth!" Mom throws her purse down. "Why do you always have to take his side?"

"Why do you never take ours?"

"Never?" Mom's voice gets cold.

"You always say you have these visions and we're supposed to do what you tell us. But you never tell us what you see. Whether they're about drinking or smoking or boys or brushing my teeth. You're like this dictator or something. For all we know, you're making it up."

"Katie, I'm a psychic. I see things."

I glare at her. "I've been smoking since grade nine. You never saw that, did you?"

"I'm not stupid, Katie. I know you smoke. Chewing gum doesn't hide anything." She takes another deep breath. "You've got nicotine stains all over your fingers."

"So do you!"

"This isn't about me!" She raises her hand.

"What are you going to do, hit me again?"

Mom grabs her plate and throws it at the sink. It misses and breaks on the countertop. Macaroni dribbles to the floor. "Stop pushing me!"

"Dad's right, you've wrecked our lives."

"I have not."

"You have, too. You and your visions. And now you've driven him away."

"That loser is a useless drunk who doesn't keep his word."

I step toward her. "He's my father."

"And I'm your mother!"

"You're a fucking bitch!"

She clenches her fists. "And you're a little liar who hates me!"

I take another step. "If you're going to hit me again, go ahead." My knees are starting to hurt. "But get one thing straight first, I don't hate you. I'm scared of you, you heartless monster."

Mom stops cold. "You're scared of me?"

"I know Dad's a fuck-up, but he's way better than you."

Mom's nostrils flare. "What do you mean by that?"

"He's never hurt me. Ever."

The colour drains from her face and she unclenches her fists. "Oh my God." She backs up against the counter.

I take another step. "I mean it. I'm tired of being scared all the time."

Her eyes widen. "I . . . I never knew."

"Bullshit." I clench my own fists but keep them down by my sides.

Mom swallows and shakes her head.

"Don't you ever fucking hit me again." A wave of calm washes over me. "Ever."

"I won't."

My knees relax. "Forgive me if I don't believe you."

"What should I do then?"

"How should I know? You're the psychic."

Mom nods, hugs herself, then opens her purse and takes out her cigarettes. She gets her lighter and lights one right in front of me. I'm about to tell her to fuck off for being so goddamn cruel when she takes the cigarette from her mouth and offers it to me.

"Is this some kind of test?"

"No."

I unclench my hands and take the cigarette. "What about your vision?"

She lights a second cigarette for herself. "Maybe it won't come true."

I take a drag and exhale slowly.

"You can't keep the money, though." Mom holds out her palm.

I know I'm pushing it, but I can't stop myself. "Dad gave it to me."

She doesn't blink for at least ten seconds. "Without his paycheque, we're going to need it for groceries, Katie." Her voice softens, "And apparently, cigarettes." Mom flicks her ash into the sink.

I reach into my pocket and count out five of the twenties.

Before she can say anything about the two I keep, the shitbox's engine starts in the driveway. Mom and I run outside with our cigarettes, but we're too late. The tail lights glow red in the dimming twilight while the hockey boys return to their game. "Tim!" Mom runs after Dad. The boys scatter out of her way. "I need the car!"

He doesn't stop.

Maybe he'll listen to me. I run out past Mom. "Dad!"

But he keeps going. The shitbox's tail lights brighten as it approaches the stop sign. The right turn indicator flashes.

Together, Mom and I stand in the middle of the street, being stared at by pimple-faced boys with hockey sticks. I take a drag. "He left."

Mom nods, flicks her ash on the road, and goes back into the house.

As Dad turns the corner, I shoot him the finger and follow her inside.

Deposition

Siéntese, Señora.
    Please, *jefe*, you've kept me waiting for over an hour. *El baño, por favor.*

Siéntese. Un hombre esta muerto.
    I need to use the toilet.

Será acusada de asesinato.
    I didn't kill Damon. *No lo hize.*

Será acusada de agresión.
    It was the girl, the one with the handbag.

Será acusada de alterar el orden público.
    Soy inocente! Ask the bartender.

Será acusada de quedarse más tiempo de lo que permite la visa.
    My visa has two more months on it. I want to contact the Canadian embassy right now, *jefe*.

No puede llamar a la embajada.
    Why not?

Deposition

No hay teléfono.
   I don't believe you.

Muéstreme su pasaporte.
   I've been told to never surrender my passport to the police in this country.

Su pasaporte, Señora.
   Doctor.

¿Qué?
   Doctor. Not *Señora*. My name is Dr. Elizabeth Wright.

Siéntace, Doctora.
   You can take my deposition when I come back.

¿Puede repertirlo?
   I refuse to wet myself.

No se mueva, Doctora.
   El baño, jefe.

¡Vuelva aquí!
   Oh, for Christ's sake, come with me then.

Sit down!
   I'm not going to run off into the rainforest. *Ten piedad de mí.*

Vale.
   Gracias. You speak English.

Usted habla español.
> Your charges are too important for a mistranslation. Perhaps another officer could help you?

La Prueba small village, not tourist resort. I only *policia* here.
> Are those menthol cigarettes?

¿Nos fumamos un cigarillo?
> I hate menthols.

You finish toilet? Go back to table.
> I want my name officially cleared, *jefe*.

You say not guilty?
> That's correct. *Soy inocente.*

Then who kill Dr. Foley?
> I told you. The girl with the handbag.

What her name?
> She never said. I don't even know your name, *jefe*.

Álvaro Ixtamer Puzul. You not know girl?
> Shouldn't you be looking for her, Officer Ixtamer?

I take *deposición* now, *Doctora* Wright. You work for Dr. Foley, yes or no?
> Damon Foley and I co-directed the excavations at Chinga'an Nahil this season.

Deposition

Dr. Foley alone before.
 Damon wanted to clear the ball courts. He needed someone to coordinate the crew.

Why you?
 I was the most qualified candidate. Could you open a window, *por favor*? It's hot and the fans aren't working.

It rain now.
 The rain is falling straight down like it always does this time of day.

Window stay shut.
 Damon's been under that sheet for a long time.

Lo siento. How you most qualified candidate, *Doctora* Wright?
 I have masters and undergraduate degrees in Mesoamerican archaeology from Trent University. I got my PhD from Calgary. My dissertation, where I focused on the new translations of the Mayan codices, was just published last fall. I've done field work at Piedras Negras, El Perú, and Tik'al. I speak a little Mayan, have a passing familiarity with Spanish, and probably most importantly, I've got big tits.

¿Cómo dice?
 Last year, Damon Foley impregnated an undergrad field assistant and two local girls. The undergrad had an abortion and transferred programs. Rumour has it Damon bought the locals off with two cases of *aguardiente*, some menthol cigarettes, and a few thousand quetzales. Obviously, letting Damon play with my tits was requisite.

Teodora Puzul Yojcom run away. María Ixtamer Puzul *tuvo un aborto.*

Maria shares your family names. A cousin?

María *era mi sobrina.*

Your sister. I'm sorry. *Lo siento,* Álvaro.

Why you work for such a man?

Chinga'an Nahil is pristine, a site that can make a career. Looters, vandals, and nineteenth-century gentleman amateurs never found it. The city was abandoned overnight, so it still contains the artifacts of everyday life we just don't find anywhere else. Incense burners, ceramic flutes, scribes' tools, even cooking utensils. Under the right guidance, the excavations here will rewrite history, correcting misconceptions and erroneous guesswork with the truth.

Dr. Foley not say site *importante.*

Unfortunately, Damon's recent work hasn't been as fruitful as his earlier efforts. For the past three field seasons he'd been focusing on the ball courts. He wanted to be the first to find an actual game ball, not just a ceremonial relic.

Why you come to La Prueba today?

This morning at eleven o'clock, I was excavating a *chultun* in Plaza Three —

¿*Chultun?*

A stone cistern for collecting potable water. I'd found the skeletal remains of an adult male inside. There had been a Jester God headband around the skull — the leather band was gone, of course, but luckily the stone artifact was intact.

Jester God?
The primary icon of Mayan royal rulership. The three-pointed headdress looks like a medieval jester's cap, hence the name. This one was carved in pyrite. It's about seven centimetres high.

Jester not Maya god.
The name itself has no cultural significance. The motif, however, is probably derived from the Olmec maize god. The three spreading leaves of a corn plant? Anyway, it's generally agreed only Mayan kings wore these headbands. They were like crowns.

This good, yes or no?
It was a discovery Damon should have made three years ago. After I'd pointed that out, he demanded, in front of half the crew, and at the top of his voice, that from then on I was to address him only as *Dr. Foley*. Then he threw my stuff out of our tent.

¿Por qué?
Well, I'd called him an amateur pot-hunter and told him to go fuck himself. In front of half the crew. At the top of my voice.

¿Cómo dice?
I told him to *métase el dedo por el culo*.

Why you say bad thing?

He'd also told me my tits were lopsided and I should consider an implant.

Es un cabrón.

Sí, él era.

¿Y después?

Damon said if I didn't shut up, he'd put me on the next flight back to Canada.

What you do?

I shut up. Someone had to protect Chinga'an Nahil.

No entiendo.

Damon was going to publish incorrect history and squander one of the most important sites in Central America. He believed Tik'al envied Chinga'an Nahil for their sports program.

¿Qué?

Chinga'an Nahil's ball courts predate Tik'al's, so Damon thought the last king sold his people into slavery to build the ball courts in Tik'al's Plaza of the Seven Temples, a much grander complex. But I'd just proved the king didn't betray his people. More than likely, raiders from Tik'al buried him alive.

Tik'al was enemy?

A political rival at the very least. The raiders had ruined every mural we've found, chiselled the name glyphs off every stela, and smashed every figurine and ceremonial mask. By putting the king in the *chultun*, they'd poisoned the water supply as well.

Why?

The answer for their hatred is still in the rainforest, but I'm sure it has nothing to do with ball courts. If I'm left to complete my work without being bothered by fuck asses like Damon Foley, I'll find that answer.

Esto es muy interesante, Doctora. You make Dr. Foley sound very bad.

I suppose Damon wasn't a complete villain. Some nights he'd place candles in the trees and play old Alux Nahual songs on his guitar for the crew. His *subanik* was nothing short of legendary. He said the key was to simmer the chillies with the tomatillos for at least ten minutes before adding the spices.

So what happen next?

Janice Weatherhead, our iconographer, said I could share her tent. I'm sorry, Álvaro, would it be possible to get a drink?

The brother of my wife own *comedor*. ¿Qué quiere tomar?

Anything, as long as it's bottled.

Óscar has case of *aguardiente*.

Aguardiente will be fine.

Aquí tiene.
    Gracias. Before Janice could help me move in, Damon told me I had to come with him to La Prueba. He said he needed supplies, right away.

You argue on way here?
    We hardly spoke for the whole five hours. After the hike to the river, we took the dugout, and except for the portage at the rapids, the trip was uneventful. Damon smoked his menthols and drank three bottles of Moza. I took photographs of howler monkeys.

You like howler monkeys?
    When I first arrived in Guatemala, I kept thinking they were jaguars. Three weeks later, Damon told everyone he'd finally figured out why I slept farthest from the door. "You know it's only the males that roar?" I was handing out Mozas to the crew. He snuck up behind me and cupped my tits. "The females grunt like pigs."

Why you take photographs?
    I was worried Damon was sending me home. *Me encanta este lugar.* I took pictures of spider monkeys, scarlet macaws, iguanas, toucans, and vulture nests, too.

What happen when you get to La Prueba?
    There were some boys playing soccer. They didn't even have a real ball, just a paper bag stuffed with leaves. I told Damon I wanted a few shots of the game, but with Damon's fixation on ball courts, he couldn't stand by without saying something.

Deposition

What he say?
    Damon told the boys they should be playing *ulama* instead of soccer. *Ulama* was the game of their ancestors. *"Bax ka wa'alik?"* they asked. Damon told them soccer was the sport of their conquerors and they should play their native game. They didn't like that very much.

You mean Maya ballgame? *Juego de pelota.*
    Sí. Juego de pelota is Spanish. *Ulama* is Nahuatl, the language of the Aztecs. *Pitz* is the Mayan term.

They not want to play?
    Damon taught them the rules. Only hit the ball with their hips. Keep it inbounds. They watched for about a minute before asking for their ball back. They called him names. *Pel-aná, tz'is awít.* Things like that.

What you do?
    I know enough not to interrupt a Central American soccer game by walking onto the pitch and stealing the ball. They told Damon to go away but he wouldn't until they at least gave *ulama* a try. They kept refusing and Damon kept insisting. Finally, this wiry kid with ripped shorts and brand new shoes, picked up the ball and very politely said *"Dyos b'o'otik."* The kid couldn't have been more than eleven. Damon held the kid's hips to show him the proper stance.

Boys play *juego de pelota*?
    The kid threw the ball at Damon's head. Everybody laughed. Me, too. At least, until the boys started yelling at me as well. I explained to them how Damon was a *kalan-tal*

and they shouldn't pay any attention. Damon had already drank three big bottles of Moza on the boat ride in, so he did smell of beer.

How you get Dr. Foley away?
    I had to drag him by his belt. The kid said his nursemaid was pulling him by his diaper. Damon got really angry at that. Who was that little *cerote* to make fun of him when he was trying to reconnect him to his own cultural heritage? I told Damon there were over twenty of them, and if he didn't shut up, we'd both get the shit kicked out of us.

He leave then?
    Sí. But the market was closed so we came to the *comedor*.

Boys follow you?
    They stayed outside. Aside from a handful of old men, the *comedor* was empty. The bartender offered us *aguardiente*, but Damon said rum was the only drink that should ever be distilled from sugar cane. He didn't ask for rum, though. He wanted a beer. He threw an American five dollar bill on the bar. "Gallo," he said. "Not a stinking Moza like you sold me last time."

What Óscar do?
    He dusted off *un litrin* of Gallo and gave it to Damon.

Dr. Foley return to table?
    He wanted his change first, so Óscar gave him ten quetzales. But Damon insisted on American money because he'd paid in dollars. That's when Óscar lost his smile and pointed out

we were in Guatemala. However, Damon wouldn't leave until Óscar put an American dollar bill on the bar.

What else Óscar do?
Nothing until the girl with the handbag came in. She looked about eighteen.

María Ixtamer Puzul?
She never said her name.

Tell about her.
She had long black hair, looked very tired, but was very pretty. She wore a light-coloured cotton skirt and matching sleeveless top. She dropped a woven handbag on a table and ordered a Moza, which Óscar brought over right away. The girl stared at Damon, like she knew him already, but not in a good way. If she was your sister, I understand why.

Could you know her again?
I would recognize her anywhere.

Doctora Wright, I hear enough.
What do you mean?

Será acusada de asesinato.
I told you, the girl did it. María did it.

No creo que Maria haya estado aqui. Creo que usted lo hizo.
Oh Christ, no. Please put your handcuffs away.

Será acusada de alterar el orden público.
    Soy inocente! Why aren't you listening anymore?

Llevaste a Damon al partido de fútbol. Será acusada de agresión.
    Yes, but I didn't kill him. *No lo hize.*

Será acusada de quedarse más tiempo de lo que permite la visa.
    Ahora lo entiendo. Maybe it wasn't María after all.

Was girl María, yes or no?
    It doesn't matter. This was all Damon's fault.

Yes or no?
    No. Please, put the handcuffs away and let me tell you what happened.

Vale. How this fault of Dr. Foley?
    After I'd pointed out the girl, Damon asked me, rather loudly, if I'd seen her tits.

¿Puede repertirlo, por favor?
    Sus pechos.

Es mejor muerto.
    Estoy de acuerdo contigo. I told Damon to keep his voice down, but he wouldn't stop. He said they were nice tits. Round. Full. Evenly matched. I should take a picture. Then he got up and went to tell the girl how nice her tits were.

What girl do?
    She screamed *tz'is awít* and spat in Damon's face. Damon laughed so she slapped him across the cheek. Hard.

She hit Dr. Foley first?
    ¿Es importante? Maybe Damon hit her first.

Tal vez. What Dr. Foley do after he slap girl?
    He said "Fuck ass? You Mayans can't even swear right. The expression is 'fuck you'." He said this in front of the whole *comedor*. At the top of his voice. Then the girl screamed *tz'is awít* again so Damon pushed her to the ground. "You're just a stupid Mayan hillbilly who can't take a compliment."

What you do while this happen?
    I suggested Damon and I go to the Casona de la Selva and get a room for the night. We could buy our supplies when the market opened in the morning.

He go?
    He called me a lopsided bitch and said if I didn't shut up this time, I'd be lucky to get a job digging ditches with the Ministry of Transportation. He went back to his beer.

¿Qué hizo?
    What could I do? I sat down and watched him drink.

What other people do?
    Óscar helped the girl off the floor. The old men lowered their eyes and twirled their bottles of *aguardiente*.

Then what happen?
> The girl took a handgun from her bag. It was big, either military or police issue.

What Dr. Foley do?
> His back was to the girl.

And you?
> I told Damon to turn around and apologize to the girl as quickly and as sincerely as he could.

Dr. Foley apologize?
> No. He told me any one of a hundred other dirt bunnies could do my job. They might not give head as well as I did, but at least their tits wouldn't be lopsided. I could find my own way to the airport.

Es incomprensible.
> *Sí.* Then the girl shot Damon.

¿Estás segura?
> No, wait. I closed my eyes and someone shot Damon. I never actually saw the girl do it.

Bueno.
> By the time I'd wiped Damon's blood from my face, everyone was gone. Óscar, the girl, and the old men. You came five minutes later and told me to sit here while you looked around.

Deposition

You go to airport now?
    I'd prefer not to. Chinga'an Nahil deserves the truth, the crew need a director, and my visa's still valid.

I ask one time more, could you know girl if you saw her again?
    No, I could not.

I think we understand one another, *Doctora*. I take you now to Casona de la Selva. Go to market *por la mañana*. Then, go back to Chinga'an Nahil when you ready.
    Entiendo. Gracias, Álvaro.

Relevance

June 16, the Second Sunday after Pentecost

If I keep my eyes shut, I can pretend my church is still filled with kneeling congregants fervently focussed on my words, complete with muffled coughs and creaking pews, shifting backsides and stolen whispers. I raise *The Book of Alternative Services* above my head. My bishop, Karen Vaughn, assured me its updated language was more accessible than the thirty-years-out-of-date copies of *The Book of Common Prayer* I'd finally recycled six months ago. However, I can't maintain the fantasy — my chancel smells like mouse shit layered with a thin veneer of lemon furniture polish. I lost half of my remaining congregation over the prayer books. I open my eyes and look to the ceiling where a solitary bulb burns from the rafters. Paint curls from the walls of the nave. Behind me, Christ, John, and Matthew flank the altar in their cracked stained glass windows. I have seven congregants left: Joan Young, my rector's warden; her seventeen-year-old nephew, Jared, my lay reader; Vic and Linda Newcombe, who once oversaw the kitchen; Rob Bonner, the people's warden; his wife Pat, the last of our altar guild; and seventy-five-year old Stan Dunlop, our bookkeeper.

I lead us through the Gloria Patri. Our previous exodus occurred when I supported same-sex weddings. Before that, the crisis had been female ordination. And before that, the remarriage of divorced persons. Changing a prayer book seemed such an inoffensive matter.

I amen, offer an alleluia, then continue with an Antiphon. Today is my sixty-first birthday. Both my white alb and green stole are threadbare. I recite an Invitation to Worship.

As everyone kneels, the narthex door opens at the back. Traffic noise intrudes, along with the thrum of a lawn mower and the bluster of a passing crow. A moment later, a sun-leathered woman in her late twenties, wearing torn jeans and a stained halter top, steps inside and crosses herself. She's Hispanic, dark, and pretty — as out of place in Dolsens as an NDP campaign sign.

Everyone turns to look.

"Please, join us." I beckon the woman closer.

She closes the door, dampening the sounds of the outside world, and approaches Stan's pew. "*Ayúdeme.*"

Stan lowers his eyes and flips ahead in his prayer book.

"*¿Habla usted español?*" Her voice is a droning alto.

I see neither ink nor track marks on her arms, and her black scuffed boots are free of the field dirt most seasonal workers track across town. I descend from the chancel. "Welcome to Saint Richard's. I'm the Reverend Nathan Sandry."

Joan folds her arms. Vic and Linda whisper to each other. Rob Bonner checks his watch. Pat shakes her head.

The woman's shoulders tense.

Jared smiles. "*¿Puedo ayudar con algo?*" He's done summer missionary work in Guatemala since he was twelve. Today he's wearing ripped jeans and a dark T-shirt with a silk-screened message proclaiming *It's your duty*.

Joan clutches his sleeve. "She's probably Catholic."

Jared furrows his eyebrows. "Do you want Father Nathan to lock the door?"

I close *The Book of Alternative Services*. "Do you speak English?"

She advances along the faded carpet. "*Hablo un poquito.* Little. *Ayúdeme.* Help me."

My heart skips a beat.

Jared jumps to his feet. "*¿Cómo se llama usted?*"

Joan presses her lips together. A package in yellow gift wrap sits beside her purse.

Vic and Linda Newcombe stare. Rob Bonner smirks. Pat rolls her eyes. Stan wipes sweat from his forehead.

The woman pauses.

Jared grins. "*Hola. Me llamo* Jared Young. *Esto es mi tía,* Joan."

"Jared," Joan whispers.

The woman nods to Joan. "*Buen día. Me llamo* Imelda. My name Imelda Herrera."

Joan points to an empty pew in front of the Bonners. "*Señorita*, please, you're disrupting our service."

"*Señora. Estoy casada.* I marry. My husband die."

"Forgive me." Joan slides over to make room, tugging on Jared's sleeve to do the same.

Relevance

Imelda nods twice, marches forward, genuflects, then sits beside Jared, who gives her a copy of *The Book of Alternative Services*.

Joan turns to me. "Shall we continue, Reverend?"

Pat Bonner holds up her prayer book.

Outside, a police siren waxes and wanes along Grand Avenue. Imelda tenses. I return to the chancel and begin Psalm 24.

Imelda whispers urgently with Jared until Joan pinches him and shakes her head. Meanwhile, no one else is participating in the service either. The Newcombes are sitting forward, trying to overhear the conversation. Rob Bonner has pulled out his cell phone. Pat is looking to the rafters. Stan reads ahead.

I'm losing them. I hurry through the psalm and deliver the doxology.

Reflexively, everyone amens, even Jared and Imelda, who continue their whispers.

A path to relevance might be presenting itself. I smile and address Imelda directly. "Are you in danger?"

She swallows. "*Ay-say-ell-ay* look for me."

I shake my head. "I'm not familiar with — "

"ECL," Jared translates. "It stands for *Ejército de Colombia Libre* or the Army of Free Colombia. They're leftist rebels trying to overthrow the government."

Imelda nods. "*Sí*. Colombia."

Joan tsks. "Please, continue the service, Reverend Sandry."

I hold a palm up to forestall Joan. "Why are rebels looking for you?"

"I escape kidnap."

My heart flutters briefly and I take a deep breath to calm myself. I was diagnosed with atrial fibrillation five years ago and consequently, I take a daily dose of anti-arrhythmics and blood thinners.

Jared's eyes widen. "My parents were kidnapped. They'd gone to see the ruins near La Prueba."

Joan presses her lips together. "Can't we do this later?"

Before I can mollify her, Jared turns on his aunt. "Seriously? They died there."

Imelda crosses herself. "They shoot my husband."

Vic Newcombe whispers into Linda's ear. Rob Bonner must be texting. Pat holds up her prayer book again. Stan flips another page.

The Lord helps those who help themselves, but I can't afford to alienate the faithful I have left. "Your aunt is right, Jared. It's time for your reading." I straighten and indicate the polished brass lectern, shaped in the form of Saint John's eagle on whose outstretched wings the Bible rests.

Joan relaxes. "Thank you."

"Fine." Jared jumps up and marches to the lectern, quickly finding his place in the open Bible. "A reading from Genesis 28, verses ten to seventeen. Jacob left Beer-sheba, and went toward Haran. And he came to a certain place, and stayed there that night, because the sun had set."

Outside, the lawn mower stutters — most likely having run over a stone. It sounds like a muted gunshot.

Imelda faces the door and rises.

Jared looks to me. "Father Nathan?"

I step forward. "Imelda, please wait. We're almost finished."

She pauses.

"Please."

"*Vale.* Okay." She genuflects again and sits in the pew behind Joan.

I nod to Jared then hurry through The Lord's Prayer.

Joan slams her book shut. "Not again."

The Newcombes stare, open-mouthed. Rob Bonner tucks his phone into his jacket. Pat reaches for her purse. Stan is still reading ahead.

I give the Dismissal.

Everyone amens.

Joan pushes her prayer book into its slot on the pew rail, grabs her purse and her package and marches up the nave. When she reaches the narthex, she turns. "Jared? Apparently, it's time to go."

Stan scurries out behind her.

Jared stays at the lectern. "I want to help Father Nathan."

Joan presses her lips together again. "Suit yourself."

I rush up the nave, excusing myself as I brush by the Bonners. "Joan, I hope I haven't offended you, but the Lord's work must be done on His schedule, not ours." I offer my hand.

"No reading? No sermon?" Joan lets me shake her hand. "I was both baptized and confirmed in this church. My parents' marriage was consecrated here and my brother and his wife were buried from here."

I'd performed the double service myself. I look back and see Imelda eying the door again. I release Joan's hand. "Go in peace."

Joan hands me the package, turns, and throws open the door. "Happy birthday."

I hold it open for my other congregants as Joan marches to her white minivan parked at the curb. The smells of early summer greet me — cut grass and yeast from the ethanol plant on the west side of town. A taxi turns onto Grand Avenue from the Queen Street Bridge. Even though she lowers her face, I'm sure the tousled-haired passenger with the dark sunglasses is Carol Anderson, our former choir director.

∽

June 17, Monday

FINALLY THE CLOCK TURNS NINE. For the past hour, Jared and Imelda have been huddled on my office chesterfield as I wait for Citizenship and Immigration Canada to open. I'm wearing clericals and a tweed jacket; Imelda is in her clothes from yesterday; and Jared, who insists his exams are over, has exchanged T-shirts for one branded *What have you done today*. He doesn't leave for Guatemala for another two weeks.

I navigate a labyrinthine electronic menu and endure twenty-six minutes of admonitions to stay on the line to maintain my call priority before I finally reach a human — an overburdened-sounding man who tells me his name is Michel. With his thick Québécois accent, Michel gives me his ID number and tells me my call may be recorded for quality assurance. I speak as quickly and succinctly as I can. "This is the Reverend Nathan Sandry of Saint Richard's Anglican Church in Dolsens, Ontario. I'm calling on behalf of Mrs. Imelda Herrera of Colombia. We'd like to apply for refugee status."

Michel asks for circumstances.

Imelda's hand finds Jared's knee and he reddens.

Relevance

I reach for the tin of homemade chocolate chip cookies on my desk — Joan's birthday gift to me. I give them to Jared and motion for him to share. "Mrs. Herrera was the victim of a kidnapping in her native country."

Imelda withdraws her hand as Jared passes her the cookies. "I go back they kill me."

Michel tells me a Mrs. Imelda Herrera has already made an application that was rejected. He asks if she's still in Canada.

"She's sitting with me now."

Michel clicks his keyboard then asks how she got into the country. I turn to Imelda.

"¿Disculpe?" She stuffs a cookie into her mouth. Last night, I'd gotten her a room at the Vintage Suites Hotel. The three of us shared dinner in their downstairs café before I drove Jared home. I had the soup of the day, Jared a burger, and Imelda ordered the bacon-wrapped tenderloin with fingerling potatoes.

I speak slowly and enunciate. "How did you get out of Colombia?"

Imelda swallows. "I fly from Bogotá."

"To Toronto?"

She shakes her head. "Miami. Bus to here."

Citing a Third Safe Country Agreement with the United States, Michel tells me she's ineligible for refugee status. He provides the number for the Canada Border Services Agency in case I'd like to try them, but he isn't optimistic.

I thank him and end our call.

Imelda takes another cookie.

"They say you should have either applied for refugee status in Miami or else flown directly to Canada."

Jared straightens. "That's bullshit."

I dial the number Michel gave me. "I'm not giving up."

After more menus and a protracted hold time, I reach another human — Sandeep. I don't catch his ID number. I introduce myself and describe our plight, confirming yes, Mrs. Herrera came to Canada through the United States and yes, I'm aware of the Third Safe Country Agreement. I then ask if there isn't any leeway, not even on compassionate grounds, but he says no and lists my remaining options. I thank him and hang up.

Jared returns the cookie tin to my desk.

"Imelda has fifteen days to leave Canada. From the day they first rejected her."

Jared furrows his eyebrows. "When was that?"

Imelda stands and walks to the window. "Three weeks."

I join her. A Dolsens Transit mini-bus rumbles by, its seats mostly empty. "We still have two legal options."

Jared stands as well. "What are they?"

I extend a finger. "One, we apply for a pre-removal risk assessment, although they're sure to say no because of the Third Safe Country Agreement." I raise a second finger. "Two, we ask for Imelda to stay on humanitarian grounds. But she'll have to return to Colombia until they make their decision."

Imelda shakes her head. "ECL kill me."

"And we must present a certificate of departure as proof of compliance. There is no appeal."

Jared swears.

Imelda shrugs, grabs another cookie and marches out the door. "¡Ni modo!"

Relevance

My heart skips twice. I rush out and catch Imelda by the photo gallery of past rectors. "There is a third option."

She pauses. "You say two before."

I smile. "You could stay at Saint Richard's."

She frowns. "*¿Disculpe?*"

"Sanctuary?" Jared comes up behind me. "Cool."

I nod. "You can have my office. I'll get you a cot." I usher her back and grab a pen from my desk. "We'll need groceries, toiletries, clothes." I find a notepad in my middle drawer. "Books, magazines, a television. We've got a washroom." I start making notes. "I want you to stay here."

Jared points out Saint Richard's doesn't have a shower.

Imelda eyes widen. "Vintage Suites?"

I shake my head. "I'm afraid you won't be able to leave the church until this is over."

Imelda frowns.

"I really want to help you." I offer up the tin of cookies. "Please?"

Imelda reaches for another cookie, shrugs, and turns to Jared. "*Vale.* Okay. I stay."

～

June 22, Saturday

TWO YELLOWED PORTRAITS — QUEEN ELIZABETH AND Prince Phillip — flank the stage in the parish hall, mementos from a royal visit to Saint Richard's in the 1960s. The air smells of crisped bacon and decades-old floor wax. Earlier, everyone had helped set up the stacking chairs and tables. I stand and address my congregation. "We'll begin as soon as the breakfast dishes are cleared."

Jared piles plates on an old bus cart. His T-shirt reads, *God helps those who help others.* Joan is at the table closest the stage.

Imelda, who's put on a floral sundress and sandals donated by Linda Newcombe, sits next to me. "What if they say no?"

"This is simply a formality. My bishop says I'm not canonically required to get their permission." I sit. "Though I do wish you'd let us call a press conference."

"*¡De ninguna manera!*" Imelda scowls. "I tell you no. And if only formality, why ask at all?"

"Public opinion is so very important. It can help sway the government."

She shakes her head.

Linda comes by with coffee. Pat and Rob Bonner have claimed their own table. Stan Dunlop sits by himself in the corner.

When Jared takes his seat next to Joan, I thank everyone for coming, and stand again. Linda grabs a chair at the back near the kitchen. Vic leans against the wall behind her, a dishrag in his hands, a chef's apron tight across his paunch. I raise my arms in benediction. "Let us pray."

Everyone falls silent.

I recite the Occasional Prayer for a Synod — the most appropriate prayer I can think of — and lower my arms. "Today, we make a very important decision. As you know, Mrs. Imelda Herrera has come to Saint Richard's seeking shelter from persecution."

Everyone's eyes fix on me — Jared's hopeful; the Newcombes', curious; the Bonners', dubious; Joan and Stan's, reluctant.

I take a deep breath. "However, simply because she came through the United States on her way to Canada, our government refuses to help her."

Rob Bonner clears his throat. In his secular life, he's both a lawyer and a trustee for the Board of Education. "Pardon me, Reverend, but what's that got to do with Saint Richard's?"

Jared coughs into his hand, not trying hard enough to obscure the word *asshole*.

Joan pinches his elbow.

I shake my head at Jared and present my most tolerant smile to Rob. "If we allow Imelda to be deported, it is very likely she will be killed."

Pat whispers to her husband, loud enough to be overheard. "It's like that family from Rwanda ten years ago."

I'd lost eighteen congregants over that failed sponsorship.

Linda Newcombe frowns.

"They wouldn't even convert to Christianity."

Rob Bonner sips his coffee.

Vic folds his dishrag and tosses it into the kitchen.

Pat rolls her eyes. "And the father had AIDS."

Stan nods.

Jared raises his hand. "Father Nathan, why don't you tell us more about Imelda?"

I nod. "She was kidnapped in Colombia, escaped, and has come to us for help."

Rob Bonner puts his coffee down to fold his arms across his chest.

Joan presses her lips together.

Imelda looks from Rob Bonner to Joan then turns to me. "*Padre*, I talk?"

Without the script of a prayer book or a psalter, Karen says I'm an unmotivating speaker. "Please." Maybe she'll be able to elicit some Christian charity. I take my seat.

Vic smooths his apron. Linda crosses her legs. Rob Bonner pulls out his cell phone. Pat rolls her eyes. Stan wipes sweat from his neck.

Imelda gets to her feet and surveys my congregation. "*Gracias, padre. Buenos días,* ladies and men. I know sanctuary *grande, muy grande,* and if I you, I want know who I give it to. So, let me talk about me. *No sé mucho inglés.* I not know much English, but I try tell you *todo,* all. *Vivo en Cali.* I live Cali."

Jared half rises. "Cali is southwest of Bogotá, the capital." He sits back down.

Pat stonefaces. "Thank you, Jared."

Imelda continues. "I use to live. No more. *Mi marido,* my husband, famous maker of *libros móviles.*" She turns to Jared.

Jared half rises again. "Pop-up books. For children."

Imelda continues. "One day, my husband get too rich and famous. ECL kidnap my husband, my sons, and me. They say pay *rescate,* ransom."

Linda clears her throat. "What were the names of your family, dear?"

Imelda pauses. "*No entiendo.*"

Rob Bonner raises an eyebrow. "You don't know their names?"

Joan grabs Jared and turns back herself. "This isn't a courtroom, Rob."

Imelda smiles at Joan. "*Gracias, señora.* I know names. *Llaman mi marido,* Guillermo. Guillermo Herrera."

"And your sons?" Pat prompts.

Relevance

Imelda tenses. "Manuel. Y Raul. ECL take *mi familia* over mountains into *selva*, jungle."

Rob Bonner returns to his cell phone. "Where exactly did they take you?"

Joan folds her arms across her chest. "Rob, is your knowledge of Colombian geography so complete you'd actually know where she's talking about?"

Imelda continues when I nod to her. "I not know. They make us walk twenty-eight days. I count. *Veintiocho. Poco* sleep. *Poco* food. Always walk. Always hide. From army. From American spy planes. From paramilitaries. From everybody. We walk until we get to camp. There, they torture my husband. Break all *sus dedos*."

Jared winces. "His fingers."

Imelda's voice drops. *"Me han violado."*

Pat leans forward. "What was that?"

"They rape me. In dirt before *todo el mundo*. They give *cocaína* to my sons and *se rien*, they laugh, when they sick. When that no get them money, *disparan,* they shoot my husband. When that not work, they shoot my sons."

Rob Bonner sets his phone down. "Why didn't they shoot you?"

Joan holds Jared back again. "Rob!"

Imelda answers, her voice inflectionless. "If I dead, then no money. ECL keep me for two years. When I escape *selva* and get home over mountains, I see ECL there." Imelda faces Rob Bonner directly. "I think they let me go. They still want money."

Linda looks to the door. "Are these people coming here?"

Imelda shakes her head. "Not if keep secret."

Rob Bonner nods at Imelda. "Go on, please."

"I go *aeropuerto* and take first plane. Miami. When I here in Canada and ask for help, they say no because I come through America."

Vic takes the chair next to Linda. "Why didn't you look for help in Miami?"

Imelda snorts. "Americans no like Colombians. They say we all drug lords. I lucky to find bus."

I motion Imelda to sit beside me as I stand to address my congregation. "Can I count on your support?"

Joan nods. "Yes."

"*Gracias, señora.*"

Linda nods, too. Vic smiles.

Rob Bonner holds up a finger. "What's the downside?"

Jared whirls around. "Seriously?"

Joan lays a palm on his shoulder.

I clear my throat. "There are possible consequences, Jared. Sanctuary has been given by the church for hundreds of years, but secular governments don't always recognize the practice."

Pat leans forward. "What do you mean, Reverend?"

I address the room. "Technically, we'll be breaking the law, but if we stand united in this, we can win Imelda's safety."

Rob Bonner smooths a wrinkle on his shorts. "What does Bishop Vaughn think about this?"

I step behind Imelda. "Because we've exhausted the official channels, she says the diocese will support us." Karen had also suggested I get verification from the International Society for Refugees.

Stan looks up. "How much is this going to cost?"

Linda throws up her hands. "That's your first question?"

Rob Bonner taps his table. "Stan has a valid concern. What is the financial impact? To say our congregation is struggling is a gross understatement."

I put my hands on Imelda's shoulders. "We should each help according to our own conscience. I'm willing to give up my office, but Imelda will need blankets, clothing, toiletries, and food."

Linda looks to Vic. "We have extra blankets."

Stan looks around the room. "Where are we going to find the money?"

Rob Bonner and Pat nod.

Vic, Linda, and Joan scowl and shake their heads.

Jared stands up. "What about a bake sale?"

Linda gets to her feet, too. "We could hold a raffle."

I nod. "I've heard of urban churches renting space in their steeples to telecom companies for cellular relay antennas."

Stan frowns. "We've discussed this before."

Jared folds his arms over his chest. "This is a human life we're talking about; show some fucking compassion."

Stan glares at Jared. "The finances of this church are my responsibility."

Pat rolls her eyes.

I approach the edge of stage. "I'll sell my car."

Rob Bonner leans back in his chair. "You're going to shame us into this?"

"If you're that worried about the finances, take it out of my stipend."

Rob Bonner tucks his phone into his pocket. "How can I continue to say no when you're willing to do that?"

Jared turns to Joan. "Did he just . . . "

Joan smiles up at me. "Yes."

Stan shakes his head. "Is that realistic?"

Imelda clears her throat. "*Padre* good man. *Muy* good man."

I can't back down now. Slowly, I raise my arms. "So, what do you say? Can I count on you to support Imelda's sanctuary? Can I count on you to help me save her life?"

Joan stands beside Jared. "Yes."

Linda smiles. "Us, too." Vic nods.

Stan wipes his forehead. "You've got my support."

Pat rolls her eyes and says okay.

With everyone looking at him, Rob Bonner finally nods.

∽

June 30, the Fourth Sunday after Pentecost

IMMEDIATELY FOLLOWING HOLY EUCHARIST, EVERYONE returns to the parish hall, which now smells of percolated coffee and Joan's chocolate chip cookies. Vic has made both ham and egg salad sandwiches. Linda circles with a tray, serving tea and coffee. Imelda sits next to Jared below the stage. She's wearing another of Linda's sundresses. Jared's T-shirt says *He died for you*. Carol Anderson has returned, along with a handful of others.

A triple knock at the kitchen door penetrates our communal revelry. Less than a minute later, Joan scurries into the room. Everyone quietens. She grabs my sleeve with a shaky hand. "The police are here."

My heart skips a beat.

Imelda tenses. "*¿Las chupas?*"

Carol sets down her tea. "What was that?" She's sitting next to Ray and Helen Townsend, an older couple who also disapproved of the new prayer books.

"¿La policía?" Imelda clenches a fist. "¡Hijo de puta!"

Jared furrows his eyebrows.

I touch Joan's elbow. "Please stay with Imelda."

Joan nods and takes my chair.

I smile, trying to radiate calm. "I'll take care of this." I march into the kitchen with Jared close behind to see Vic in his apron, blocking the outside door, his arms folded across his chest.

Two police officers wait beyond — a man and a woman — their dark uniforms and bulletproof vests stark against the noontime sun. Mourning doves lament from a nearby maple tree. I extend my hand and approach the door as Vic steps back. "Hello officers, what can I do for you? I'm the Reverend Nathan Sandry."

The male officer doesn't blink. "Please ask Imelda Herrera to come forward." His name tag reads M. Reaume.

When neither officer takes my hand, I step back and offer a reconciliatory tone. "I'm afraid I can't do that."

The female officer steps forward, her blonde hair gathered in a severe bun. "We're here to take her into custody." Her name is D. Giroux.

"I've granted Mrs. Herrera sanctuary."

"Doesn't matter." She crosses the threshold into the kitchen.

My heart flutters as I move to block her. "You're violating that sanctuary, officer."

Officer Giroux looks at her partner who shakes his head. She returns to his side.

I take a deep breath. "Thank you."

Officer Giroux leans forward to call through my kitchen. "Imelda Herrera? Come out here, ma'am."

My heart flutters then flips into full-on palpitations. "You'll have to send your messages through me, officers." I take a another deep breath. It's not helping. I'm starting to get dizzy.

Officer Reaume puts his hands on his hips. "Are you feeling okay, Reverend?"

Behind me, someone closes the door to the parish hall.

I look as steadily as I can into his eyes. "Yes." Luckily, my doctor has assured me atrial fibrillation isn't life threatening.

Jared and Vic move to flank me.

Officer Giroux reaches for her handcuffs. "Sanctuary isn't a legal defence, Reverend."

I've rehearsed this conversation many times this past week, anticipating this confrontation. I soften my voice and hope I don't pass out. "Please don't break the sanctity of my church. If you deport Mrs. Herrera, some very dangerous people will kill her."

She glares at me. "Not our responsibility."

Jared steps closer. "That's cold."

I try to keep from showing my disgust as I look into her eyes. Light spots dance in my vision. "You have my word, Mrs. Herrera will not leave Saint Richard's."

The police look at each other, then Officer Giroux puts her handcuffs away. "If she runs before we come back with a warrant, you'll be charged with obstruction of justice."

I put out a hand to steady myself on the doorjamb. "I understand. Go in peace."

Relevance

As the police return to their cruiser, Jared and Vic pat me on the shoulders and I close the door.

∽

August 14, Wednesday

IT'S BEEN A MONTH AND a half of getting nowhere. The police haven't been back but the government still refuses to hear Imelda's case and my savings are dwindling. Karen has been pressuring me for a press conference to renew interest in the church, even though our numbers have more than tripled. I've refused to comply until Officer Reaume called an hour ago to inform me he's been instructed to execute the deportation order. He's coming at nine tonight.

Behind me, a television camera whirrs and a young reporter with a crisp voice speaks into a microphone. "Here with breaking news is Thera Quinn, reporting live. A case of international intrigue has gone unreported in the heart of southwestern Ontario. A Colombian refugee seeks sanctuary in a beleaguered Dolsens church while the federal government demands her deportation."

I enter the church and walk down the hallway. Imelda has tacked a wish list to the notice board — she wants more movies, a laptop, and a leather jacket. A game console, too. A blue light flickers from under my closed office door. I try the knob. It's locked. Thera Quinn's voice — electronically filtered through Imelda's flatscreen — fills the air.

Imelda Herrera, wife of slain Colombian book publisher Guillermo Herrera, has been entrenched in Saint Richard's Anglican Church for the past month and a half. Once a prisoner of rebels in the South American jungle, Herrera is now battling a different foe, the Canadian government. I'm standing outside the church where —

Something big crashes and the news report cuts out. "*¡Hijo de puta!*" A light clicks on. "Yes or no, I say no press?"

My congregation should be here in fifteen minutes — plenty of time to set up before the police arrive. Karen passed on her regrets saying she wouldn't be able to make the drive from London in time. I knock.

"*¿Quién es usted?* Who there?"

"It's Father Nathan. Let me in, please."

"It your office, *Padre*. Come when you want."

"The door is locked."

A moment later Imelda opens it. Her blouse — once Joan's — is misbuttoned. Jared, who decided not to go to Guatemala this summer, is beside her. His T-shirt is inside out so I can't read its message. The curtains are pulled tight.

Jared notices his shirt and his face reddens.

Beer bottles and empty pizza boxes litter the floor. "You've been drinking, too?"

"No."

Imelda nods. "*Sí.*"

I hold up a hand. "That's not why I'm here."

Imelda scowls. "Idea of Jared, not me."

Jared whirls on her. "You called me."

"*¡De ninguna manera!*" Imelda shakes her head.

Jared's jaw drops. "You did, too."

I step into my office. "The reporter."

"No press." Imelda plops down on my chesterfield. "I no want ECL know where I am."

I close the door behind me. "The police are coming."

Imelda throws an empty bottle at the fallen flat screen Rob Bonner donated. It bounces off the broken plastic and rolls under her tousled cot. She picks up another bottle. "*¡De ninguna manera!* I no talk."

I take the bottle from Imelda and set it on my desk, which she'd pushed against the wall a month ago. "We'll protect you."

Imelda shakes her head.

Jared reaches for Imelda's shoulder. "Public opinion will be behind you. Trust us, this will work."

She throws him off. "*¡Déjeme en paz!* You know nothing!"

I take two deep breaths. "Canada is not a dictatorship like Colombia. If enough people feel a certain way about something, our government will listen."

"Colombia not dictatorship." Imelda snorts. "What if ECL hear? What then?"

Jared folds his arms over his shirt. "They're in the jungle, for Christ's sake. How can they do anything to you?"

Imelda shakes her head. "ECL more smart than you think."

I open the window. At the curb, the Newcombes climb out of a tan crossover. Carol Anderson is with them. "Talk to the reporter. Just come as far as the doorway. We'll all stand in front of you."

Imelda reaches for another bottle. "No."

Jared rubs his face. "Look, do you want to stay in Canada or go back to Colombia and get shot?"

Imelda throws the bottle at his head. "*¡Que te calles!*"

Jared ducks. "Fuck you!"

"*¡Mierda!*"

Jared clenches his fists. "Imelda, please."

Imelda looks at Jared, then glances to me. "*Las chupas* coming now?"

I nod.

Imelda scowls. "*Vale.* If we must do this, we do this."

◡

Twenty minutes later, my burgeoning congregation has joined us outside the narthex door. We number twenty-three and provide a good show of solidarity even though the streetlights make us all look jaundiced. The air smells of cooling asphalt and mud from the Thames River. Joan presses her lips together as she stands next to Jared, whose righted T-shirt reads, *He is always with you.* The Newcombes and the Townsends pass out coffees and juice. The Bonners have set up the stacking chairs. Carol Anderson sits in the first row. Stan Dunlop hasn't been to church in three weeks.

The camera waits on a tripod while Imelda and I stand behind a microphone. Imelda has combed her hair and put on a fresh sundress. Cicadas buzz from the willows.

I lead a short prayer then brief everyone on their roles tonight. If necessary, we'll link arms and form a cordon around Imelda. No one at the *Dolsens Daily News* or the local radio station picked up the phone when I called. "Let us begin."

Thera Quinn, who's wearing a red blazer over a black blouse and blue jeans, speaks into her microphone. "So my first question should be obvious. Why haven't you gone to the press before, *Señora* Herrera?"

Imelda shrugs. *"No se."*

"Let me rephrase my question. Most sanctuary claimants are eager for media publicity. You've avoided it. Why is that?"

Relevance

Imelda tenses as she points to the Thames River where a police cruiser is crossing the Queen Street Bridge. *"¿Padre?"*

I whisper "don't worry" into Imelda's ear before I address the camera. "Let's just say some undesirables are looking for her and we didn't want to draw their attention."

"What's changed your mind?"

"The police are on their way right now to execute a deportation order."

Thera Quinn glances at the police cruiser turning onto Grand and smiles wide. "How do you like it here in Dolsens, *Señora* Herrera?"

Imelda shrugs. *"Me encanta este lugar.* People here very nice. They give place to live. A bed. *Televisión,* too, so my English get better."

Everyone murmurs their approval. Vic opens a box of doughnuts. Linda sips her coffee. Linda's daughter, Donna, stands next to her husband with their infant daughter on her hip. Carol Anderson beams openly.

The questions continue. "You were once held by the ECL in Colombia, *Señora* Herrera?"

"Sí."

"Isn't the ECL, the *Ejército de Colombia Libre* or the Army of Free Colombia, in fact, considered a terrorist organization by most nations of the western world?"

Imelda watches the police cruiser pull up beside the Newcombes' crossover. The curb parking is full. *"¿Puede repertirlo?"*

I gently touch her shoulder and face her toward the camera. "Yes, Canada considers the ECL terrorists. So does the US, the European Union, and Colombia itself."

Imelda snorts. "ECL not terrorists. *Ejército del Pueblo,* a people's army."

Officers Reaume and Giroux step out of the cruiser and adjust their belts. They consult quietly.

Imelda tightens her eyes."They state of belligerence in Geneva Convention."

My heart trips.

Thera Quinn motions for Imelda to look at her instead of the camera. "Doesn't the ECL rely heavily on cocaine for funding?"

"Coca plants. A tax, only. All legal."

Rob Bonner frowns.

I release Imelda's shoulder. "And they extort ransom money from kidnappings. They held Mrs. Herrera for two years. And killed her family. They are terrible people."

Imelda shrugs. "*Sí,* kidnap happen."

"Are you a member of the ECL, *Señora* Herrera?"

"I not ECL."

"Reverend Sandry, what do you think of the possibility of Stockholm syndrome? Where hostages identify with their captors?"

"Mrs. Herrera is a victim not a terrorist."

The police step onto the sidewalk, look at the gathered crowd, and shake their heads. Officer Giroux speaks into her shoulder radio.

Imelda nods. "*Sí,* victim. *Gracias, Padre.*"

Thera Quinn presses on. "What will the ECL do when they learn where you're hiding?"

I frown. "You're aware we've avoided the media precisely to keep Mrs. Herrera's name from their attention."

Relevance

"Why is that, Reverend Sandry?"

Jared throws his hands in the air. "Because she's scared the ECL will shoot her, you stupid cow."

Joan pinches Jared's side.

My congregation murmurs. Linda puts her tray down and seeks out Vic, who puts his arm around her. Carol Anderson stops smiling.

"You feel very passionate about this."

"No shit." Jared pulls away from his aunt.

After consulting her notes, Thera Quinn invites Jared into the shot. "This is Jared Young, a dedicated member of Saint Richard's congregation. His own parents were killed during a botched kidnapping attempt in Guatemala two years ago. Tell me, Jared, do you see this as an extension of your missionary work?"

"What the fuck kind of question is that?"

Joan presses her lips together.

My heartbeat starts to flutter. "Please don't sensationalize our situation. This press conference is about stopping a deportation order that will surely result in an innocent woman's death." I take a deep breath then turn to stare down the police.

Thera Quinn spins her camera to focus on the police. The cicadas buzz on. After a quick shrug, Officers Reaume and Giroux get back in their cruiser and drive away.

Everyone cheers.

Jared smiles and hugs Imelda.

She hugs him back, but looks to me. "Yes or no, they gone?"

My heart calms. "Yes."

Thera Quinn steps up to shake my hand. "That last shot of the police retreating was incredible."

∽

August 19, Monday

I SPENT THE NIGHT OF the press conference at Saint Richard's in case the police came back. They didn't. For the rest of the week we took rotating shifts so Imelda wouldn't be left alone. Joan took Thursday with Carol Anderson — she'd forbidden Jared from seeing Imelda again. Friday, the Newcombes and the Townsends sat with her. Saturday was the Bonners, and last night I stood watch again. Now, I'm in the clothes I slept in on the chesterfield, and my office smells like warm sweat and cold coffee.

When the Immigration and Refugee Board of Canada calls, I take notes as fast as I can. I thank the caller — her name is Bernice — and give her my email address so she can forward the appropriate forms. Then, I end the call and go looking for Imelda.

I find her in the washroom running water in the sink. "Imelda, open up!" A grin breaks over my face. "Good news!"

Imelda turns off the tap. "¿*Padre?*" She opens the door and dabs her armpits with a towel. She's wearing jeans, a tube top, and her scuffed boots. "What you want?"

"We've won! The government has agreed to rehear your case!"

Imelda drops her towel in the sink. "¿*Sí?*"

I nod. Vigorously. "¡*Sí!* Yes! The Federal Court has returned the case to the Refugee Protection Division. The press conference worked."

Relevance

Imelda steps into the hallway. "I stay in Canada?"

"There's no guarantee the original decision will be reversed, but at least now we have a chance to present your story." I tell her about the hearing next week. Immigration never really considered her case before, they just dismissed it arbitrarily because of the Third Safe Country Agreement. "I don't see how we can lose."

Imelda glances down the hallway as the kitchen door opens behind me. She frowns.

I let a smile cross my lips. "And the removal order is suspended." Before I can continue, someone touches my elbow and I turn. It's Joan Young.

Her eyes are red. "The police want to see you, Nathan." She presses her lips together.

My heart skips — once, twice, three times. Perhaps they haven't been made aware of the Federal Court decision. "Imelda, stay behind me."

Joan leads the way to the kitchen door.

Officer Reaume stands on the threshold with a manila envelope in his hands. Behind him, two police cruisers wait at the curb.

I step forward to block his access to Imelda. "I just got off the phone with the Immigration and Refugee Board of Canada. They've agreed to hear the case."

Without a word, he hands me the envelope.

Inside is a press release from the International Society for Refugees. Included is a photo of a middle-aged Hispanic woman wearing rags in the jungle. I read the title and my heart skips into full-on palpitations. *Imelda Herrera released today.*

Imelda leans forward. "*¿Qué es?*"

Officer Giroux appears behind us — she must have come in earlier with Joan. "Read it, Reverend." She keeps her hand close to her belt.

"After three years of captivity, Colombian businesswoman Imelda Herrera Dávila was released unilaterally by the ECL, the Army of Free Colombia. Responding to an unsolicited tipoff from the ECL's high command, a Red Cross team flew by helicopter into the jungle near the small town of San Cipriano to collect the former hostage and transport her to Cali where she was reunited with her sister, Verónica Beltrán Dávila. No ransom was paid."

Imelda's shoulders tense. "*¡Esos malparidos!*"

I point at the picture. "That's not Mrs. Herrera."

Imelda nods. "*Sí.* Fake."

Officer Reaume shakes his head, once. "We've contacted the Red Cross in Colombia as well as the local authorities. This is genuine."

My heartbeat becomes even more erratic. "No."

Officer Giroux takes out her handcuffs and turns to Imelda. "We're here to arrest you."

Imelda clenches her fists. "*¡Padre, ayúdeme!* Help me!"

Dizziness hits me hard. "There's been some mistake."

Officer Reaume holds up another piece of paper. "We've got a warrant."

I take a deep breath. And another.

Officer Giroux reaches for Imelda. "Ma'am, you're being charged with personation with intent, drawing a document without authority, and failure to comply with a federal removal order."

Imelda pulls away and steps into my arms. "*¡Protéjame, Padre!*"

Officer Giroux continues. "You have the right to speak to a lawyer without delay. Do you understand what we've told you?"

I'm close to passing out. "I've vowed to protect her."

Imelda drags me toward the door. "*¡Cállate!*"

Officer Giroux holds up her handcuffs.

Imelda snorts and sidekicks Officer Reaume hard on the inside of his knee, breaking it instantly. He screams and falls as Imelda releases me, jumps over him, and runs out the door.

I swoon and find myself falling, too.

Officer Giroux rushes forward and catches me. "Stop her!" She lowers me to the steps.

Two additional police officers leap from the second cruiser and give chase.

Imelda sprints across Grand Avenue and makes for the Thames River. Sailboats laze in the sunshine. Squirrels scatter to nearby tree trunks.

Officer Giroux lays her palm on my forehead. "Hold on, Reverend."

But I can't. The stress is too great. I black out.

༄

August 25, the Twelfth Sunday after Pentecost

THE CONCRETE FLOORS OF THE Southwest Detention Centre reek of urine overlaid with industrial solvents. My footsteps echo as I approach Imelda's cell. Bishop Vaughn is furious.

Imelda faces the wall.

I clear my throat. "It's Father Nathan."

She doesn't react.

"Imelda?"

Imelda keeps her back to me.

The officer who escorted me in checks his watch. "Ten minutes, Reverend."

I thank him, open *The Book of Alternative Services* I brought, and recite the Occasional Prayer for Those Who Suffer for the Sake of Conscience.

It's faint, but Imelda does amen.

I close the book. "Jared is in police custody, too."

She shrugs.

"Did you hear me? He vandalized Saint Richard's. Spray painted 'hypocrites and liars' on the altar. Destroyed all the stained glass windows. Broke into my office and set fire to your things." I didn't want to press charges, but the police said it wasn't up to me.

"¿Y qué?" Her voice is a frigid monotone.

I rub my face with my palms. "Who are you, really?"

Imelda turns to glare at me. "I dead woman."

"The police tell me your name is really Luisina Tirado de Francisco. They say you're an ECL Column Commander. They say your *nom de guerre* is La Loba."

She shrugs again. "Must be true, if *las chupas* say."

I slap the bars, making the metal ring. "They say you're the one who tortured Guillermo Herrera! They say you're the one who had Manuel and Raul Herrera shot! They say you're the one who ordered the rape of the real Imelda Herrera!" My heart stays calm. "They say you laughed."

She gets to her feet. "If ECL kill me, it your fault."

"You must answer for your sins."

Relevance

"Do you know what prisons in Colombia like, *Padre*?"

I shake my head.

"They not like here. No clean clothes. No new shoes. No hot food. Only two guards for whole prison. You keep key to own cell."

"You're getting off easy."

"You no understand." She grips the bars. "The guards let paramilitaries watch other prisoners."

"So?"

"Paramilitaries massacre our people! Burn our villages! Kill our families! They hate ECL!"

"May I at least hear your confession?"

She shakes her head. "I not sorry. I have no choice, *Padre*."

"You always have a choice, Luisina." I could have chosen not to help you. If I had, Saint Richard's might still have a congregation and Jared Young wouldn't have a criminal record. I open my book to The Reconciliation of a Penitent. "Innocent blood never goes away. But if you honestly repent, if you get down on your knees and beg God to forgive you, He will."

She tenses. "You right, I choose. I choose ECL over life in dirt. I choose to carry gun. I no want rape every time soldiers come over mountain. ECL, army, paramilitaries. All same. Drugs. Kidnaps. But ECL say women equal of men. No one else say that. Everyone else kiss CIA boots. I not ask God to forgive me for ECL. ECL save me."

"The ECL kicked you out for your atrocities." I hold the page with my thumb. "Make your peace with God."

Luisina crosses herself. "It all one. God destroys both good and bad. That in Bible."

She's right, it's from Job 9:22. Maybe everything is futile. Nothing I've ever done seems to be relevant. Not the prayer books, not the family from Rwanda, not my ministry, and most definitely not my misguided plan to offer sanctuary to a terrorist and bring people back to the church. "I'm sorry, Luisina."

"I sorry, too, *Padre.*"

Her eyes widen as I detach my clerical collar and tuck it into *The Book of Alternative Services,* but she does accept it when I offer it to her. "Go in peace."

Mercy Manor

I stop at the base of Mercy Manor's derelict grand staircase to catch my breath. It's about an hour after sunset on a Friday night in early June and everything reeks of cat pee and rotting carpet. Graffiti splatters the walls.

"Keep moving, Janie." Crystal runs upstairs with our only flashlight. Crumpled candy wrappers skitter across the floor. Something hisses in the darkness below, probably in the basement.

I scramble up after her.

On the third-floor landing, Crystal whirls and splashes light on her face. "I'm a ghost. *Whoo.*"

I shiver. "Not funny."

The flashlight goes out.

Crystal swears.

The floorboards creak, but at least I don't hear any more hissing. I duck my head in Derek's football jacket to escape the smell.

Crystal slaps the casing — once, twice. The flashlight stays off. She enters the closest room and beelines for the window to shuffle the batteries. The window glass is long gone. When the flashlight still won't turn on, she swears again and abandons it on the windowsill.

I step into the room behind her. Twilight glints on discarded beer bottles. A soiled mattress hugs the far wall. Gungy shag carpet covers the floor. This must have been one of the bedrooms. I poke my head out the window and let Derek's jacket fall to my shoulders. Outside smells like river mud and yeast from the ethanol plant on the far side of town. "Now can we talk?" Cicadas buzz in the nearby willows.

Across the river, muscle cars and four-by-fours fill the McCrae House's lit parking lot. Mr. Turner, our socials teacher, has been trying for years to get the Dolsens town council to close the bar and designate the building an historic site from the War of 1812. He's also been trying to save Mercy Manor. It used to be Dolsens only home for unwed mothers and was run by an order of nuns from Montreal.

Crystal puts her arm around my shoulder. "Of course. We shouldn't waste this rare opportunity." She feigns absolute astonishment. "But where is Mr. Hoekstra?" Crystal can be such a turd sometimes.

"Grounded." I scan the McCrae House for Derek's two-tone pickup, just to be sure.

Crystal drops her arm. "I should have known." She slips a mickey of vodka from her jeans and unscrews the cap.

"I'm your best friend."

Crystal takes a drink and looks unconvinced.

I try to smile. "What's wrong?"

"You really want to know?" When I nod, Crystal sets the vodka on the windowsill next to the dead flashlight. "You've turned into an epic cling-on." She ticks off her fingers. "Math,

English, socials, spare, detention. You haven't gone anywhere without Derek Hoekstra's hand on your ass for the past four months."

I abort my smile. "I didn't know it bothered you."

Crystal makes kissy faces and rubs herself. "Ooh, Derek. I haven't seen you in ten whole minutes. I missed you so much. Take me now."

"Cut it, will you?"

"You're even wearing his clothes." Crystal pokes Derek's senior championship patch from three years ago. "Have you picked out a china pattern yet?"

I pull Derek's jacket tight. "He gave it to me last night." It's almost the truth. "I really need to talk."

Crystal smirks and folds her arms across her chest. "We had all detention to talk."

"Detention was a gong show." Mr. Turner was late. Ashford Wilson posted upskirt porn to the Internet. Megan Ladd booby trapped erasers with chalk. Crystal inked stars on her wrists.

Crystal puts her hand on my shoulder again. "We could have talked at the liquor store."

I pull back. "The clerk was being a total perv and you had to snap my bra." In the parking lot, a girl laughs too loud. It could be Megan, although I can only see a silhouette. The Thames is narrow here and the McCrae House is less than the length of a football field away. During the War of 1812, Mr. Turner says the local militia single-handedly captured the American garrison occupying Thomas McCrae's property. It was the very first all-Canadian military victory ever.

"At least he didn't card you."

"He's never like that when Derek is with me."

Crystal reaches into Derek's jacket pocket and grabs my cigarettes. "I'm not your backup."

The girl who might be Megan kneels in the grass and pukes loudly. People groan and back away. I hold my hand out for a smoke.

Crystal slides my lighter from my cigarette pack. "You know the nuns buried the dead babies in the yard, don't you?" Without taking a cigarette, she closes the pack and returns it to Derek's pocket.

I fold my arms across my chest. "Cut it."

Crystal holds the lighter close to her chin and ignites it. "Dead baby ghosts. *Whoo!*" Her shadow flickers on the ceiling.

Something black hisses in the overgrown grass directly below the window.

Oblivious, Crystal steps over a desiccated condom and bounces across the mattress to examine the wall.

I push the dead flashlight off the windowsill. It lands with a crash. The something black bolts for the river. I hope it was a cat.

Crystal reaches under the mattress and pulls out a can of spray paint. She aims it at the wall and sprays for a few seconds until the can sputters and dies. "Prick." Crystal tosses the can into a corner.

"What are you doing?"

Crystal lets the lighter go out. "Nothing."

I step on the mattress and grope my way to her side. "Show me." I find Crystal's hand in the dark and take back my lighter.

"Janie, don't."

I flick on the flame. She'd been trying to blotch out some of the words from *Crystal Reaume Swallows*. "Who wrote that?"

She grabs my lighter and lets the flame go out. "How should I know?"

"But why would — "

"I said I don't know."

The people in the parking lot start laughing again and the cicadas buzz louder. After a minute, I say, "So, what I wanted to ask you — "

"Later." Crystal reignites the flame and scratches the paint with her fingernails. "Help me get this off."

I join her, but our scratching isn't doing anything. "We need something else."

Crystal keeps scratching anyway. "See if the shovel they used to bury the babies is still here."

"You're not funny."

Crystal points at the wall. "Neither is this."

I glance through the window to the grass below. It's pitch black. "They never buried any dead babies down there."

Crystal jumps off the mattress and kicks fallen ceiling tiles out of her way as she searches for something to remove the graffiti. "Would you focus?"

"They would have taken them to the cemetery." The moon peeks out from behind a cloud.

"Duh."

In the silvery moonlight, I scan the room. All we have are broken tiles, candy wrappers, empty bottles, the condom, and the discarded spray paint can. "We could get more paint."

Crystal gives me her don't-be-a-moron look. "We're not leaving until this is gone."

Last night, before I stole his jacket, Derek and I accidentally knocked a wine bottle and two glasses from his mom's night table. They shattered and scratched the shit out of the hardwood floor. When his mom got home, she spotted the damage right away. She grounded him and kicked me out. I pick up a beer bottle and smash it against the windowsill. "Try this." I give the biggest shard to Crystal.

Crystal scrapes at the paint. After two minutes, she ignites the lighter and frowns. "I can still read it." She throws the shard into the corner where it plinks against the spray paint can.

I step back and try to find something else. Stained and pitted linoleum peeks through the decomposing shag carpet. I'm not sure what colour it once was. Mouldering yellow wallpaper sticks to the wall like a rash. I think it was a floral pattern, or maybe vines. Whatever it was, it's hideous. An empty light socket dangles from the sagging ceiling. "I wonder what it was like for the girls who had to live here."

"Those morons have to be wrinkled grannies by now." Crystal lets the lighter go out and returns to the window. "Or they're dead." She picks up the vodka and takes a sip.

"I bet they were really scared."

"Maybe they're ghosts." Crystal reignites the flame close to her face. "*Whoo!*"

"Cut it." I grab the lighter from her. "What could they have done?"

Crystal gives me her don't-be-a-moron look again. "There have only ever been two options, Janie. Keep it or get rid of it." She puts the vodka back on the windowsill, snatches back my lighter, and returns to the wall. She holds the flame to *Crystal*

Reaume Swallows and tries to burn it away. The paint darkens, but we can still read it.

From somewhere below, I hear the hissing again. I shiver. "This place freaks me out."

Crystal brings the flame close to her face. "*Whoo!*"

In the parking lot across the river, an older woman laughs like a horse. Some guy yells "fuck." It sounds like Ashford Wilson. I wonder if Megan will be puking on the Internet tomorrow. "Accidents happen."

"To morons." Crystal lets the lighter go out.

"Hey, condoms break."

Crystal takes another drink. "Did Derek knock you up?"

I shake my head. "No." Last week, Derek poured rum on the barbeque. The flames jumped with a whoosh. I grab the bottle and splash vodka over *Crystal Reaume Swallows*. "Try it again."

Crystal ignites the lighter and we wait for the whoosh. It doesn't come. Crystal swears again.

I put the vodka back on the windowsill.

"I'll have to lift more paint." She looks like she's going to cry. "Let's go to Quigley's."

We've already been there tonight. Mrs. Quigley would get suspicious and call the cops. "We do this now." I try to smile again.

"Why?"

"There's no way I'm going to let people know you swallow." I go to put my right arm around her shoulder, but she pulls back.

Crystal scans the wall. There're over ten different blotches. She shakes her head. "Fucking prick."

"You know who wrote all this shit?"

Crystal shrugs.

"Before, you said you didn't."

"I lied."

"Who was it?"

"You really want to know?"

I nod.

Crystal drops her eyes to the floor. "Your sperm donor."

I put my hands in Derek's pockets. "Why would Derek write that about you?"

"Last Saturday." Crystal traces her name with her finger. "You were at your mom's down in Windsor. He came over."

"You hooked up?"

Crystal nods.

I rip off Derek's jacket and throw it at her. "You bitch!"

Crystal lets the jacket fall. "Boys are like batteries, Janie. Just pop in a new one."

I grab Crystal's chin and force her to look at me. "He's the only boyfriend I ever had who lasted longer than two weeks."

"He's been spraying these walls ever since you started going out."

"You're bragging?' I glare at her.

She shakes her head. "Most of them were about you." Crystal's eyes dart from right to left.

"Why didn't you tell me?"

Crystal blinks. "You haven't spoken to me in four months."

"And that gives you the right to fuck him?" When she doesn't respond, I slap her hard across the cheek.

Crystal's eyes widen but she still doesn't answer.

I slap her again.

A tear brims her left eyelid. "It didn't mean anything."

I slap her a third time.

The tear dribbles down Crystal's cheek. "Okay, I'm a shitty friend and a backstabbing whore." Crystal looks to the wall and readies herself for another slap.

My gaze flicks to the graffiti and I lower my hand. "I'm such a moron." I clutch my stomach.

Crystal's eyes leap to my face. "You're pregnant."

I shrug. "I think so. I don't know. I'm late. Ten days."

"But you said before — "

Now it's my turn to give her a don't-be-a-moron look. "I lied, okay?"

"Does Derek know?"

I shake my head. I was going to tell him last night.

Crystal bites her lip. "For the record, I only gave Derek a blow job. I never slept with him."

I wipe my eyes with my sleeve. "Whatever."

"Janie, please. I'm really, really sorry." Crystal reaches for my hands. "You're the most important person in the world to me."

I push her away. "Then stop sucking off my boyfriends."

"I promise, never again." Another tear rolls down her cheek.

We've been together for over ten years, ever since Crystal punched Megan Ladd in the stomach for pulling my hair in kindergarten. "Help me get back at Derek."

"What if you're pregnant?"

"He cheated on me. Fuck him."

"Okay." Crystal wipes the tears from her cheeks with her thumb. "Public humiliation. A good beating. Everyone will hate him."

"From now on, no one touches Derek Hoekstra. Not me, not you. Not anyone. Got it?"

"As of this moment, he's a born-again virgin."

I look to my flat stomach. "And you'll help me figure out what to do, if I am."

"I won't leave your side. Ever."

I pull Crystal into a hug. "Then we're cool."

After a minute, she whispers. "Are you going to keep it?"

I step back. "I don't know."

"You're going to have to decide soon. And tell both your parents. And you're going to have to — "

I put my finger to her lips. "All I want from you is unconditional support. Got it?"

"Okay." Crystal reaches for my hand. "Let's get a test kit from Quigley's. You rearrange the magazines." Mrs. Quigley is a little OCD. It's how we distract her to get our cigarettes.

But *Crystal Reaume Swallows* is still on the wall. I shake my head. "Not yet." Derek poured rum on an already-burning barbeque — he didn't try to light the alcohol first. Maybe that's what I did wrong. I take the lighter from Crystal and set fire to a corner of the mattress. Crossing my fingers, I drizzle vodka over the flames. They brighten right away. This could work. I empty the bottle and fire flashes up the wall, curling the wallpaper and charring the drywall. Within a minute, *Crystal Reaume Swallows* is gone.

Crystal smiles. "Thank you."

The room glows orange as the flames spread. Heat washes over us. We have no way to put out the fire.

Across the river, a car horn sounds. People start to yell.

At least no one will ever see Derek's graffiti again. I toss his jacket into the flames. "Fucking prick." His championship patch starts to melt.

"Hold on." Crystal rescues Derek's jacket as the fire reaches the ceiling.

"What are you doing?"

Crystal gives me her best evil-villain smile. "Everyone knows Derek wasn't at the McCrae House tonight."

I look out the window. More people are leaving the bar and joining the crowd in the parking lot to stare at Mercy Manor. I return her smile.

"So, Derek's virginity starts now." Crystal pushes his jacket out the window. "The fire department will find it."

I grab her hand and together we run for the stairs, the roar of the fire growing fast behind us. Thick smoke fills the landing. We hold our breath and scramble down as quick as we can. Everything gets dark on the second floor and from there we have to grope our way. Finally, we reach the ground floor and the smoke clears. In the distance, sirens wail. As Crystal drags me toward the back door, I look back to the basement stairs and hope the cat got out.

Dal Segno al Fine

AFTER FIVE FAILED ATTEMPTS TO close his zipper, Raymond Townsend swears at his numb left hand and shuffles his new walker out of the apartment's bathroom. He works his way around two suitcases and a cardboard box labelled *R. Townsend, Shoes* waiting by the front door. Ben's keys lie on the floor beside the box, and the door is wedged open with yesterday's *Dolsens Daily News*. Raymond pokes his head into the outer hallway. It smells faintly of urine and the beginnings of today's lunch feature — Salisbury steak. "Ben, wha~ is this?" Raymond knows he sounds *abafando*, muted and muffled like he's chewing marbles. When Ben doesn't respond, Raymond kicks the newspaper into the hall and lets the door slam shut.

Across the hall, Mrs. Thane raises the volume on her television — an infomercial for walk-in bathtubs. Next door, Mr. Gaglioni sings something lustful in Italian.

Raymond kicks Ben's keys between the suitcases then shuffles to the sliding glass door where a safety railing forms an ersatz balcony. Their apartment is on the fourth and top-most floor. To the south, the midmorning sun glints off the windows of Dolsens General Hospital where Raymond has spent the past six weeks. On the sidewalk below, a smoking girl in tight pants pushes a stroller. An unleashed dog lifts his leg on a maple tree. Ben's rented minivan is parked in the retirement community's loading zone. The little shit must be moving him again.

From the bedroom, Helen asks "What am I supposed to do?" Her voice is *energico,* as strong and clear as the day Raymond married her fifty-seven years ago. That day, she'd worn a floor-length white satin gown with two strands of her mother's pearls.

Raymond forces a smile and faces the bedroom door.

Helen enters carrying her purse in her left hand. She's dressed only in her shoes and yesterday's underwear. Her gait is proud, erect, and poised, hindered only by the bewildered expression on her face.

Raymond drops the smile and tries his best to enunciate. "Pud your clothes on, please."

Helen twists her right hand in a quarter circle — two, three times. "What am I supposed to wear?"

"The blouse and skir~ I picke~ ou~ for you." With his unresponsive hand, it had taken Raymond half an hour to set aside the cream silk blouse and tweed skirt Helen had worn to their joint retirement party where the philharmonic had presented them with a joint retrospective of their recorded work. Raymond hadn't even known Ben was in the apartment this morning.

"I beg your pardon?" Helen's voice chills.

Raymond speaks slowly, *lento.* "Blouse and skird. On the bed."

Helen marches into the bedroom, heals clicking over the laminate hardwood like a metronome. "Is Raymond out there?"

Raymond turns back to the sliding glass. "I'm Raymon~." Below, Ben paces between the rose beds and the minivan, his hands-free phone plugged into his left ear. He presses one of Raymond's hatboxes to his hip.

"I know that. The other fellow." Helen enters the living room again, her expression stern. "You know who I mean." She's wearing the blouse but not the skirt.

"Pu~ your skir~ on."

"I beg your pardon?"

"Skird."

Helen returns to the bedroom. "He used to live with us."

Raymond blinks away a tear. "~homas passe~ las~ year." His kid brother had been only fifteen when Raymond had seen the signs and been forced to condemn their parents to a nursing home; their mother had dementia, their father a failing heart. At the time, Raymond and Helen were twenty-two, newlyweds, and recent graduates of the Royal Conservatory. Thomas stayed in their spare room until he graduated college with a diploma in business administration.

"I'm not talking about your brother, dummy."

Ben stops near the minivan and pats his pockets with his free hand.

"I mean the other one." Helen returns, this time, fully dressed. She's even put on a strand of pearls. She approaches the suitcases and brushes her fingertips over each one. "He was supposed to be here."

Raymond grips his walker. "You knew abou~ this?"

Ben gives up on his pockets and looks up to the apartment. Raymond retreats into the shadows.

"Oh, Raymond." Helen's face darkens. "Your thingy's undone."

"Wha~?"

"Your . . . your . . . you know, your thingy."

"I nee~ a reference, Helen."

She points at Raymond's crotch with a crooked finger and a look of disgust. "That."

Raymond sees his open fly and considers his next trip to the bathroom. "Jus~ leave i~."

Helen reaches for Raymond's zipper. "He says I'm supposed to help."

"Who says? Ben?"

"That's his name." Helen's voice crescendos. "Ben says I'm supposed to help when you piddle!"

Mrs. Thane ups her volume again.

Raymond grimaces. "Please, keep your voice ~own."

Mr. Gaglioni repeats his chorus, but is falling flat. A vacuum starts at the far end of the hall — Joan is early today.

Helen continues. "Because of your . . . your . . . "

"My wha~?"

"Your . . . " She wiggles her fingers. "These things."

"My han~s?"

Helen digs a balled tissue out of her purse and dabs at Raymond's pants. "Yes." At their first public performance, she'd removed a drizzled mustard stain from Raymond's tuxedo jacket moments before they took the stage. After that, Helen's dab check had become part of their preconcert routine. Raymond had been concertmaster — principal first violin. Helen played piano. That first night, they'd nailed a Mendelssohn double concerto and received their first standing ovation.

Raymond gently pushes her hand away.

Helen folds her arms across her chest. "You hit me."

"I barely ~ouche~ you."

Helen's right hand starts to twist. "You hit me."

Raymond closes his eyes. In the nursing home, his mother would publicly accuse his father of the vilest abuse — punching her arm, slapping her face, pinching her breasts — all of it untrue. "Shi~."

"Now you're swearing at me!"

Raymond opens his eyes and pitches his voice *tranquillo*, as soothingly as he can. "Please, nod so loud."

"Ben says you're not supposed to swear." Vehemence shakes her words, like the night she told off Thomas for accepting a job in Indiana. She was so mad, she'd even yelled at him in her sleep. At their concert the next day, Raymond had been so upset, he'd started to miss notes. The conductor demoted him to second chair mid-performance. Later, their GP diagnosed a transient ischemic attack and warned of the likelihood of future strokes. The demotion had been permanent.

"Ben can go ~o Hell!"

Helen glares at him until the telephone rings. She darts forward and picks it up. "What do you want?" Her agitation fades. After a beat, Helen knits her eyebrows. "What keys?"

Raymond shuffles his walker forward, snatches the phone, and yells into the receiver. "You're a sneak!" After three failed attempts, he gets the handset in its cradle.

"Why did you do that?"

Dal Segno al Fine

His father could sometimes refocus his mother by playing one of her favourite records. Raymond doubts he could fit a CD into the player with his hands they way they are, so he tries a different approach. "I~ was a wrong number."

"It didn't sound like a wrong number." Helen regards the phone for a moment, then says "I'm supposed to use that for emergencies." Bewilderment clouds her face.

"This isn'~ an emergency."

Helen opens her purse and takes out a folded paper. "Press two, then talk." She holds the paper so Raymond can see it. "See? He wrote it down." Helen had always recorded appointments and birthdays on whatever was at hand — calendars, business cards, and occasionally sheet music — possibly an early indicator of Alzheimer's. During their Scottish tour, she'd defaced the conductor's score of Haydn's *Symphony No.97 in C major* with multiple copies of Ben's new phone number in Calgary.

Raymond closes his eyes, breathes deeply, then opens them again. He pitches his voice tenderly again. "Are you hurd?"

Helen shakes her head. "No."

"Do you need anything?"

"I don't know."

Raymond bites his lip. "Think aboud id."

Helen creases her forehead. After a moment, she looks up. "I don't think so."

"Then everything is all righ~. No emergency."

"Are you sure?"

Raymond forces another smile. "Yes."

Helen refolds the paper and is just about to put it back in her purse when the phone rings again. Instantly, she snaps back to *agitato*. "Who is that?"

Raymond answers the phone. "Why ~on'~ you go home?" He gets the handset down on his second try.

The paper vibrates in Helen's hand. "Who was that, Raymond?"

"Wrong number again."

"People are so stupid. They're not supposed to call the wrong number."

The phone rings a third time.

"Shi~," Raymond says.

Helen shifts the paper to her left hand. "You swore at me."

Raymond picks up the phone and slams it down, unanswered. "I was swearing a~ tha~ s~upi~ thing." He offsets the handset in the cradle and tries a new tactic. "Have a sead."

Helen refolds the paper. "I beg your pardon?"

Raymond points at their oak dining table. They'd bought it in New York. The table lies halfway between the living room and what the retirement community calls a kitchen — a kitchen with no oven, no stove, or even a toaster. "Sid."

Helen puts the paper back in her purse. "He was supposed to be here."

Raymond steers Helen to the table. "Please." He slides a chair back for her.

Helen sits and her gaze settles on the suitcases and the *R. Townsend, Shoes* box. "He said he was taking us to the new place today."

Raymond takes a deep breath. "No." As a child Ben had preferred Junior Achievement to learning an instrument. Any instrument.

Helen opens her purse and unfolds her paper. "Two then talk. No, that's not it." She takes out a second piece of paper. "Mapleview Gardens, ten o'clock."

Raymond checks the clock on the wall — 9:45 AM. He reaches with his right hand. "Show me." When Helen gives him the paper, he crumples it and throws it at the suitcases. "No fucking way. Nod me."

"You swore at me."

"You wen~ behin~ my back."

Helen's right hand twists. "He gave that to me."

Raymond closes his eyes. "The paper was blank."

"It was not."

Raymond opens his eyes and pitches his voice as level as he can. "You're nod remembering properly."

Helen quietens. Eventually, the bewilderment drains from her face. "What am I supposed to do now?" She looks to Raymond expectantly.

"Are you hungry?" Raymond shuffles his walker to the mini-fridge and opens the door. Inside are two plastic-wrapped sandwiches, a bruised apple, a piece of sugar-free lemon pie, and two Styrofoam cups. There's also a white paper bag from the hospital.

Helen points to the floor. "We're supposed to eat downstairs."

Raymond closes the mini-fridge. "The ~ining room's no~ open ye~."

Helen looks at her stomach then sets her purse on the table and stands. "Maybe I am hungry."

Raymond opens the mini-fridge again. "We have the ~wo chicken-sala~ san~wiches you brough~ back yes~er~ay. An~ an apple. An~ some pie."

"I'll have one of those." She joins him at the mini-fridge.

"Which?" Raymond always liked pecan pie. He hasn't had it in years, though — doctor's orders.

"Don't be stupid. One of those." Helen grabs both sandwiches. She takes them to the table and unwraps the plastic. Without waiting for Raymond, she picks up a dirty plastic spoon and digs into a sandwich.

In the nursing home, his father had spoon-fed his mother until the day she finally refused to eat. From then on, he'd held a cup to her lips until she hit it away. Raymond grabs the paper bag with his right hand and closes the mini-fridge. "I ~on'~ wan~ a san~wich."

Crumbs fall from Helen's open mouth. "This is like . . . "

Raymond shuffles to the table and sets the bag down. "~on'~ use the spoon, Helen."

Helen nods once and sets the spoon down.

Raymond mimes eating a sandwich with his hands. "Like this."

"That's just stupid." Helen picks up the spoon and works it into the bread again.

Raymond touches the spoon. "You ~on'~ nee~ tha~."

"Stop speaking like a dummy." Chicken salad gloops down her lip.

Raymond shakes his head and sits. "Fine. Ea~ i~ however you wan~."

Dal Segno al Fine

Helen gouges out more sandwich. "This tastes like where we used to go."

Raymond lets his eyes wander over the apartment. Framed photos with visiting soloists. A score signed by Orff. His first Strad in a glass shadow box. A photo of Helen and Thomas squinting into the sun in front of the newly constructed Roy Thomson Hall. Ben will probably sell them all except for the last photo. "Reference, please."

"That place you're supposed to wait in line."

Raymond opens the paper bag. His pills are inside. "A res~auran~?"

Helen shakes her head. "No."

"The I~alian marke~?"

"Don't be such a dummy. Where we used to go."

Raymond closes his eyes. "A ho~el?"

Helen slams her spoon down. "You don't have it right! I went there all the time!"

"Please, lower your voice." Raymond opens his eyes. "The thea~re?"

"Yes." Helen nods and relaxes. "No. Before we did the thing."

"The Symphony Bis~ro?" They'd stocked a passable Pinot Noir and their pecan pie was sublime, but they'd experimented too widely with their pheasant salad, baked brie, and pimento sandwiches.

"That's right." Helen scoops another bite of sandwich. "This is fucking cold."

Raymond takes a deep breath and removes a blister pack of pills from the paper bag. His mother's profanity filters disappeared, too. "Woul~ you ge~ me some juice, please? I~'s ~ime for my me~s."

"What did you say?"

Raymond speaks slowly. "Please, ged me a juice."

Helen stands and marches to the mini-fridge. She grabs the two Styrofoam cups and brings them back to the table. She gives one to Raymond, keeps the other for herself and sits down.

Raymond grips the blister pack and slowly pushes the pills out, his unresponsive left hand making the task as difficult as performing the harmonics and arpeggios of Ernst's fourth variation on "The Last Rose of Summer". Three days' supply pops onto the table. "Shi~."

"You swore at me."

"No." Raymond pitches his voice *tranquillo* again. "I swore ad me."

Helen reaches for the pills. "What are you supposed to do with those?"

Raymond pushes her hand away and accidentally knocks the paper bag to the floor with his left hand. "Shi~."

"You swore at me."

Raymond closes his eyes. "S~op saying tha~."

Helen points at the pills. "Where did you get those things?"

The nurse had given him the bag yesterday when he'd been discharged. Raymond opens his eyes and bends to retrieve the bag, holding on to the table with his right hand. "They sai~ I'm suppose~ ~o ~ake them." Raymond's left hand can't grasp the bag.

Helen stands. "Why?"

Dal Segno al Fine

"So I'll ge~ be~~er." Raymond accidentally pushes the bag under his chair, but not far enough to reach with his right hand. "Woul~ you help me?" He straightens.

Helen gets up, grabs the bag, and sets it on the table. "What are they, Raymond?"

"The ~oc~or sai~ they were ~o keep me from having more s~rokes." Raymond pushes his pills for the day into his mouth — three small white ones, two tiny pinks, and a thick two-toned capsule. He swallows the whites and the pinks without a problem, but the capsule gets stuck in his throat. He sips at his juice — pulp-free orange — but it backs up his throat. Raymond coughs. "Shi~!" Before Raymond can clear the capsule, there's a knock at the door. "An~ ~ouble shi~!"

"You swore at me." Helen looks to the door and stands.

Mrs. Thane turns her television up to maximum — she's now learning about stair lifts. Mr. Gaglioni switches to a minor key, but pitches it sharp. Joan's vacuuming is still far away.

Raymond, who's still coughing, says "Jus~ leave i~."

"Don't be stupid." Helen marches to the door, her heels clicking across the laminate.

"Are my keys in there?" It's Ben.

Raymond staggers to his feet. "Helen, ~on'~ open i~." The capsule is slowly dropping.

Helen's right hand twists. "What am I supposed to do?"

"Si~ ~own." Raymond grabs his walker and shuffles forward.

"Mom?" Ben calls through the door.

Helen grabs the doorknob.

"No!" Raymond coughs again.

"Is this an emergency?" Helen marches to the telephone and picks up the handset.

Ben knocks some more. "Let me in!"

The capsule finally clears. Raymond closes the safety latch on the door.

"I'm supposed to call if it's an emergency." Without dialling, Helen puts the phone to her ear. "Hello?"

Raymond takes a deep breath. "Pu~ tha~ ~own."

Helen hangs up. When Ben knocks again, she marches to the table and grabs her purse, accidentally knocking her juice over Raymond's pills.

"An~ shi~ again!"

"You swore at me!" Helen opens her purse and takes out her paper. "Two, then talk." Helen returns to the phone and presses two buttons. "Two, then talk."

Ben's cell phone rings in the hallway.

Raymond closes his eyes. "Shi~, shi~, shi~."

Ben answers his phone. "Mom?"

Helen speaks into the handset. "What am I supposed to do?"

Raymond opens his eyes and shuffles to Helen. "Give me tha~."

Helen continues to speak into the phone. "I thought you were supposed to be here."

Raymond snatches the handset and hangs it up.

Helen's hand twists into a spastic blur. She used to play with such precision, even De Schlözer's *Étude No. 2 in A flat*.

Ben speaks through the door. "What's going on?"

"You're a sneak!"

Ben's voice softens, *diminuendo*. "We thought it would be better this way."

Helen opens her purse. "It's on the paper."

"You both need round-the-clock nursing and I've got to get back to Calgary. I've been away too long."

"Wha~?" Raymond takes a deep breath.

Helen rummages in her purse.

"I've been here for a month and a half. Mom and I put the application in three weeks ago. Mapleview had to move people so you could be together."

"Las~ ~ime, you sol~ my house withou~ ~elling me!" The kid had stayed with Helen while he'd been in hospital after his first stroke. That time, Ben had asked the government to take away his driver's licence and found them the apartment that was supposed to have everything.

Ben softens further still, *pianissimo*. "I know this isn't easy."

"*Dal segno al fine*," Raymond whispers. From the sign to the end. Raymond cannot repeat his father's hell. He sees the ruined remnants of the pills then shuffles back to the table and opens all the blister packs, separating the capsules from the viable whites and pinks.

Ben knocks again.

Helen approaches Raymond and pokes his shoulder. "What am I supposed to do?"

Raymond glares at her. "You were in on this."

"I'm scared."

Raymond shakes his head and continues to separate pills.

Helen pokes Raymond again. "I'm losing my words."

Raymond shakes his head. "You've go~ pills for tha~."

"I beg your pardon?"

Raymond takes another deep breath. "I said you've god pills for thad."

"Will yours help me?" Helen sweeps up a handful of white and pinks and stuffs them in her mouth.

"No!" Raymond knocks the pills from her hands. They skittle over the table and scatter across the floor. "Spi~ them ou~! Now!"

Helen spits out the pills. "You yelled at me."

Ben knocks again. "Open the door!"

Raymond points at Helen's chair. "Si~!"

Helen sits in her chair and her eyes well up. She hasn't cried since Thomas' funeral. Heart attack. They'd driven to Fort Wayne to retrieve his body. Her right hand blurs.

Raymond considers what's left of the pills. Too many whites and pinks have been lost to overdose.

A tear rolls down Helen's cheek. "You yelled at me."

Ben slaps the door one last time. "I'll be right back." His footsteps retreat down the hall. The vacuum stops.

"And you cheaded on me." Raymond closes his eyes. "Ben isn'd mine."

"You knew?"

Raymond opens his eyes. "You ~alk in your sleep."

Helen wipes her cheek with an open hand. "I didn't know you knew."

"This you remember?"

A key slides in the lock and the door opens partway, caught by the safety latch. Ben pushes his face into the crack. "Hey, let me in."

Dal Segno al Fine

Helen wipes another tear. "I don't know what I'm supposed to do, Raymond."

"Mr. Townsend?" Joan calls from the hallway. "Is everything all right in there?" Mrs. Thane opens her door, her television blasting on full. Mr. Gaglioni shuts up.

"I don't have time for this," Ben says.

Raymond switches his attention to the ersatz balcony with the safety railing.

Ben kicks the door. "Open up, now!"

Raymond shuffles his walker to the sliding glass door.

Helen twists her hand. "What am I supposed to do, Raymond?"

Raymond points at Ben. "Your son will ge~ you."

A look of disgust clouds her face. "Oh, Raymond, your thingy." She starts to get up.

"Jus~ leave i~." Raymond opens the sliding glass door. Cicadas buzz in the rose beds. A mourning dove plaints from the maple. Muted traffic rumbles by. The smells of car exhaust and tree pollen fill the apartment.

Raymond grips the safety railing with both hands. "Helen?"

"Yes, Raymond?"

Raymond enunciates clearly one last time. *Risoluto.* "Open the door." He waits until Helen releases the safety latch then, when he's sees Ben coming in, he leans as far as he can over the railing and lets go.

Waiting for the Defibrillator to Charge

Gentlemen, put your hands together and welcome our next lovely lady to the stage. Making her Doll House debut tonight, this is Destiny.

My buddy, Zak, extends his beer bottle for clinking. "Welcome home, Mike."

I touch my bottle to his and thank him for the ride. It's good to be back. My other buddy, Josh, usually drives, but his sister Jess has the car tonight. Zak showed up with his dad's pickup, and although three guys on a bench seat can be a little close, it's better than taking the bus. Zak said Josh's coffee-shop suggestion wasn't worth considering so he told him to shut up — he was taking us to the Doll House like they'd originally planned. Josh sulked and played with the door lock until Zak told him he'd have to pay for it if he broke it.

I clink Josh's bottle and ask what Jess is up to.

Josh swigs his beer, tells me she had to work, and looks away.

Before I left Mississauga last June, the four of us went to the movies together. Zak bailed and took Josh with him when I picked a drama, but Jess said she had fun even though there was only one flashed tit, no ass worth mentioning, no one said *fuck*, and nobody got their asses kicked, not even the shithead who deserved it. Jess is the kind of girl who drinks Coke for breakfast. She and I were going to phone each other over the summer, but I didn't and she didn't, and now it's September and it's too late. I'll have to call her tomorrow.

Zak tosses his empty cigarette pack on the table. "Got a smoke?"

I don't know how the Doll House gets away with it, but they're completely lax on the whole non-smoking thing — which is good because Zak, Josh, and I like to smoke while we drink and watch naked women dance. Us and all the suits and the bikers and the workers from the autoplant. The tables are full and the air conditioner is working overtime.

Josh buttons his jean jacket up all the way. Behind him, a black-haired girl passes by, her nipples making little tents in her top.

Zak taps the table and leans close to me. "Give me a cigarette."

Aerosmith's "Rag Doll" booms from the speakers as a new girl takes the stage. I try to check her out but Zak's big head is in my way.

Here she is, boys. Enjoy the show and keep your hands out of your pants.

"Cigarette." Zak snaps his fingers.

I take out my new pack, still wrapped in plastic. I search for my lighter, checking all my pockets, but I don't find it. "Got a light?"

Zak grunts and takes the cigarettes.

I haven't smoked much lately. It's not that I'm trying to quit — I'm not — I've just been living with my Aunt Linda and Uncle Vic in this small town called Dolsens, where there aren't many places to smoke. Dolsens doesn't have a strip club, my aunt's a public health nurse, my uncle sells cars and knows everyone, so it was just easier to avoid any inevitable scenes. My aunt and uncle are pretty cool for people in their fifties, though — when they heard I was going to fail grade twelve chemistry again, Aunt Linda offered to help me with summer school. My parents made me give up the city lifeguard job I'd lined up with Zak, but living in Dolsens wasn't all bad. With my aunt's help, I finally passed chemistry and graduated high school.

Gentlemen, I can't hear you. Show your appreciation and make some noise.

Zak tosses a cigarette to his lips and slaps the table.

My beer bottle wobbles. I steady it and turn to Josh. "You want a smoke, too?"

Josh doesn't react — he's looking at the back of the club so he must be scoping out the girls hustling lap dances. I don't think he can hear me over the music.

I like the Doll House, but honestly, I'd have rather gone to Josh's coffee shop tonight where it would be quiet enough to have a conversation. I wanted to tell him and Zak and Jess about my summer — about how my Uncle Vic let me drive a Dodge Challenger, about how he took me to Detroit for a ball game, and about how cool my aunt was to get me a volunteer job in the Dolsens General Hospital emergency department. I even got to use the defibrillator once — although it's nothing like the movies where patients give a giant convulsion and come back to life. This older guy was having a heart attack and the intern had me attach the gel pads to the guy's chest and back. Together, we got his heart beating properly again. It was one of the scariest things I've ever done, but also one of the coolest. I actually got to help save someone. A stringy brunette brushes my arm on her way to the bar. Her skin is warm and she smells like coconut.

Zak watches me check out the brunette. He smiles. Josh is still focused on the back of the club.

I'm not sure if I could explain Dolsens to these guys, anyway. Having deep conversations isn't something we've done a lot of.

The brunette notices me looking at her. She puts in an extra wiggle and continues on her way.

Come on, you deadbeats, clap for fuck's sake. Let Destiny know you're out there.

I shake my head. What was I thinking? A coffee shop? I've been away too long.

Zak takes out his chrome lighter and, with a double flick on his jeans, opens and ignites it. He sucks in the flame and clicks his lighter shut. Zak and I met in cadets five years ago, but unlike Josh and me, he's lost interest in joining the regular forces. The doctor found a heart murmur so he failed his recruitment medical in May. Zak's grown his hair out over the summer. "You missed out on a good thing, Mike," he says.

"What's that?"

"I signed on with the city full time. Benefits. What's your big plan for the future?"

"They said I could reapply as a med tech if I passed chemistry."

Zak stuffs his lighter in his pocket and focuses on a blonde grinding her ass into this guy's lap at the next table. Zak's head is blocking my view of the stage, but I catch a glimpse of a skinny girl with long blue hair wearing a gold bikini. She's riding the brass pole.

Yeah, that's the way, Destiny. You sure this is your first time?

Josh, who's red hair is buzzed short, turns back to the table. I reoffer my cigarettes and he takes one. Josh is signed up for the basic military qualification course in October. He isn't thinking about any specialized training — he's wanted to be an infantry soldier ever since we were in grade one — back when we chased little Jess around their backyard with our Nerf guns. Josh scoops the bar matches from the ashtray, lights one, and holds it out for me, his hand a little wobbly.

"You okay?" I ask. Josh is normally sniper steady.

"I haven't eaten yet. Maybe we should get a pizza." Josh starts to get up.

Zak flicks his cigarette in the ashtray and glares at Josh. "You owe me."

Josh glares back at Zak but speaks to me. "Just hurry up before my fingers get burned." He sits back down.

I light up and move my chair so I can see the blue-haired girl, but Zak moves in front of me. I shrug and lean close to Josh, shouting so he can hear me over the music, "Summer school wasn't that bad . . . " The table shifts under my weight and I lift my elbows to rebalance it.

Looking good out there, Destiny.

Josh starts to say something, when Zak leans in close. "It's time."

Josh shakes his head, grabs his beer, and looks at his lap.

"Yes." Zak slaps the table and it shifts again.

My bottle falls and spurts foam at me. I grab it, rescuing maybe a third of my beer. "Time for what?"

Zak pivots and flourishes his arm like a showman, pointing at the stage. "See for yourself."

Cold beer rains on my lap and I look down. "Damn it, Zak." I back my chair up and wipe my jeans with my hand.

"Look at the stage."

"In a minute."

Zak takes my bottle. "Now."

My pants are soaked. I glare at him.

He points at the stage.

With Zak's head out of my way, I see the blue-haired girl's face for the first time and my senses quit on me. After a moment, I shake my head and my vision returns. The skinny girl in the gold bikini twirls and her blue hair spreads out like the superhero cape she wore when she ran from our Nerf bullets. A flash of red reveals her true hair colour beneath an incomplete dye job. Jess grips the brass pole with one hand and spins to the floor.

Slowly, my other senses return — drums pound through the speakers; the mixed scents of coconut lotion, beer, and smoke haze the air; cold wet denim Cling Wraps my legs.

Jess pushes her breasts together and purses her lips. She's seventeen and way too young to be in this place, no matter how wild she thinks she is.

A factory worker with a dirty ball cap pushes a blue bill into her G-string.

You in the hat in pervert's row. Sit down. You're blocking our view of the lady.

Zak laughs, slowly.

Josh slouches and peels the label from his beer bottle.

I crouch behind Zak so Jess won't see me. "We should go." I look for the front door, but it's a long way away, on the far side of the lap dancers. No one is looking at them anyway — everyone is focused on the stage. All the suits and the bikers and the factory workers are clapping and whistling and cheering. My cigarette burns my fingers. I stuff it in the ashtray.

Zak sets my bottle on the table. "Welcome home, Mike." He's not smiling anymore.

I turn to Josh. "You're just going to sit there?"

Josh keeps his head down.

My eyes drift back to the stage.

Jess grips the pole again, this time with both hands and hangs upside down, her legs forming the inverted chevron of a private's rank insignia.

You're a pro, Destiny. You've had lessons, haven't you?

Josh still refuses to look at me. He picks at the torn label stuck to his bottle.

I tell him I'd never look at my sister naked.

Josh's ears burn red.

I try to laugh but can't. I need to get out of here. "Coffee? Pizza? A movie? Whatever. My treat." I duck lower behind Zak.

Josh looks at me with cold eyes. "Too late now, Mike."

Zak laughs again. "We're not done here."

"What do you mean?" I ask.

Zak puts two fingers to his lips and whistles.

Jess's head swivels. She finds Zak and then stares right at me. My senses almost quit again, but I keep them with me by focusing on her eyes. I'm hanging on to see how she'll react — it's like waiting for the defibrillator to charge back in Dolsens Hospital — all focus and dread and extreme apprehension. She holds my gaze for a few heartbeats and then slowly, deliberately, winks her left eye. She pinches her nipples through the gold triangles of her bikini and mock gasps.

I think I just came in my pants. Anyone else?

Heat rises in my ears. All I can smell now is spilled beer. "Let's get out of here."

Zak slides his chair back, exposing me to the stage. "I'm not going anywhere, remember?"

"What?" I stand up.

"You heard me."

I shake my head. Somehow me passing chemistry has turned into a betrayal. I don't need this. "Josh, you coming?"

Josh scrapes the last of the label from his bottle. "I didn't drive." I don't know what Zak's got over Josh, but it's enough to keep him here.

Gentlemen, like all of our gorgeous ladies, Destiny is available for a personal lap dance right after her show.

Zak folds his arms across his chest. "Your girlfriend didn't tell you about her new job?"

I glare at Zak and reach for my cigarettes. "She's not my girlfriend."

"No?" Zak doesn't blink.

Josh slides my bottle toward me. "She'll be done soon."

On stage, Jess grabs herself with both hands.

"I'm done now." I stuff the cigarettes in my pocket and turn my back on them. I take the matches, too. I thread my way through the crowd, heading for the front door. My wet jeans itch. It takes me two tries to find a clear path, but when I reach the exit, I look back. Beyond the suits and the bikers and the factory workers, Zak stares at me, his head low like a pit bull. Josh peels the label from my abandoned bottle.

Give her a big round of applause. Thank you, Destiny, we're all ready to do you now.

Jess's second song starts. She unclips her top behind her back.

I step outside and the sudden silence buzzes in my ears. The air is warm and the smell of exhaust hangs heavy. I reach for my uncle's keys but I don't have them — I'm not in Dolsens anymore.

I light a fresh cigarette and walk away, following the sidewalk along barred storefronts washed in the yellow glow of the street lights. A city bus passes me and stops for a red light. The nearest bus stop is just past it, in front of an all-night pizza place. I drop my cigarette and start to run.

Rage

294

Dolsens, Ontario. A late-May sun rises over the squat brick homes lining Partridge Crescent. The thrum of air conditioners fills the air, competing with the static of buzzing cicadas and the plaints of mourning doves. Every third house runs a sprinkler. Maturing ash trees offer cooling shade. A stray collie sniffs its way along the wheeled garbage bins set out at the curb. The wind — a light breeze — is from the south, so the effluent from the ethanol plant isn't falling over town today. Although just barely six o'clock, the air is already humid and heavy with the smells of corn pollen and wet grass. Dark towering clouds threaten the horizon.

Ten year old Kevin Ladd rides his bike from house to house, a bag of newspapers slung low over his shoulder. He's tall for his age with dusty blond hair that's long overdue for a trim.

Keeping pace in blue crops is his mother, Teri. She's tall, lean, and handsome and has tucked her blonde hair through the back of a tight-fitting black ball cap.

Two houses away, the collie raise its leg on a local election sign set low to the ground.

"Cut it out!" Kevin angles his bike to intercept.

The collie startles and retreats under a fence.

Kevin pops a wheelie then returns to circle around his jogging mother. "You looked way nicer than the other people giving speeches last night."

"Thank you."

"Are you going to ground Megan again?"

Teri times her pulse against her watch. "She had a bottle of gin in her purse."

"Good thing Dad didn't find it."

"He's doing pretty good this time. 293 days sober." Kevin pedals ahead as Teri pauses by the urine-spotted election sign. Like the majority of the signs here, it reads *Re-Elect Teri Ladd, School Trustee*, and comes complete with a professional photo.

Two blocks east on Robin Lane, a grey Dodge Journey pulls up to a tan brick house with white vinyl siding. A blue Toyota Prius and a black convertible MGB Roadster fill the driveway. The Journey's passenger door opens and bass beats throb into the morning air as black-haired Megan Ladd spills out in mud-splattered running shoes. Her knuckles are wrapped in a pair of men's briefs. Kim Robbins, Megan's best friend, keeps her foot on the brake. Although hard to see on her dark skin, Kim has a freshly given black eye. Both girls wear torn hoodies and dirty cut-offs. Megan grins. "The look on Five-Hole's face when she caught us boning her boyfriend. Hilarious."

"I think she's going to be a little distracted tonight."

"Boys are so stupidly useful."

Kim blows a kiss and guns the engine. "Skank."

"Ho." Megan waves as the Journey screeches away.

Rage

The sky darkens and the storm clouds break from the horizon to close in.

~

Kevin has four papers left. "Go easy on her, okay? It's tough being a teen." He races up another driveway.

"It's not so easy being a mom, either."

Kevin puts a paper in the mailbox. "I hear you."

Teri sips from her water bottle and winks at her son.

~

Megan slips off her muddy shoes and tucks them under a pair of rubber boots by the kitchen door. The table is set with four bowls. Fresh-brewed coffee waits in the machine. A whiteboard on the fridge reads *293*. Megan sneaks into the carpeted hallway to listen outside the closed master bedroom door. She hears snoring.

~

Lightning forks across the sky. Kevin places his last newspaper in a mailbox and pedals back to his mother.

Teri points at the roiling clouds. "Race you back?"

Kevin grips his handlebars. "Loser gets wet."

"Loser makes breakfast!"

~

Megan runs the water in the shower. She unwraps the underwear from her hand and drops it to the floor. Her knuckles are split and bleeding. In the medicine cabinet, she has to move a bottle of laxatives to get to the hydrogen peroxide.

~

Teri and Kevin race down Pheasant Drive, then veer onto Cardinal Crescent. This part of town is known as Birdland. They pass more election signs, most of them Teri's.

As the first raindrops hit the ground, Kevin cuts across a lawn.

"Cheater!"

Kevin jumps the curb. "Sorry."

Teri sprints to pull ahead of her son. "Muesli and yoghurt!"

Kevin grunts and stands on his pedals. "Pancakes!"

~

Megan steps into the tub and rinses bubbling peroxide from her split knuckles. Purpling bruises cover her forearms.

~

Kevin enters the kitchen as rain splatters the windows. He keeps his voice to a whisper. "I win."

Teri puts her hands on her knees and gulps air. "You had a bike."

"You've got longer legs."

Rain pummels the driveway outside.

Teri closes the door. "Pancakes it is."

Kevin pumps his fist. "Yay!"

"Shh." Teri points down the hallway to the master bedroom.

Kevin cups his hand over his mouth and tiptoes to the fridge. He takes out the maple syrup and places it on the table.

~

Megan turns off the water and reaches for a towel. Finding the rack empty, she steps out of the tub and bends to open the cabinet. As she pulls a folded towel from the top of the stack, an oversized hardcover book wedged within falls to the floor.

Rage

The book is *Intimate Photography*. Its cover is a shadowed and entwined nude couple, presented in black and white. Megan opens the toilet tank and drops the book inside. Displaced water sloshes over the porcelain.

~

As Teri sets out flour, sugar, and baking powder on the counter, Kevin finds Megan's muddy running shoes hidden under the rubber boots. He tries to hide them better, but Teri sees them anyway. Her smile fades.

~

Lightning flashes outside. Megan winds her wet hair in a towel and bundles her clothes in a ball.

~

Teri stalks down the hallway, her footfalls silent, her breath held. She taps her fingers lightly over the bathroom door.

A cupboard closes within.

She tries the doorknob. It's locked. "Megan, open up." Her voice is a strained whisper.

The bathroom door opens and Megan steps out, wrapped in a second towel. She slips her hands behind her back.

Distant thunder booms. The lights flicker.

Teri pushes her way into the bathroom. "Were you out all night?"

"I'm just up early. Big game against the Rangers today."

Teri flings open the cupboard and muddy clothes tumble to the floor, the men's underwear on top. "What's this?"

Megan leans over Teri's shoulder. "Looks like underwear."

"Whose are they?"

Megan shrugs. "Dad's?"

Teri looks closer at the briefs without actually touching them. "Is this your blood?"

"Why would my blood be on Dad's underwear?"

Teri sniffs the air. "Have you been drinking?"

"Nope."

"I smell alcohol."

In the kitchen, Kevin scrapes a chair across the linoleum. Teri cringes.

Megan looks her in the eye. "Dad's secret stash?" She keeps her hands behind her back.

"On your breath. Show me your hands."

Megan presents her hands, palms up, forearms down.

"Not funny."

Megan rolls her eyes and flips her hands over to reveal her split knuckles and bruised forearms.

"Well?"

Kevin rattles around in the cutlery drawer.

Teri winces again.

"These girls from DCI jumped Kim and me. I think they were drunk."

"You're grounded."

From behind the closed door of the master bedroom, a male voice bellows. "What's going on out there?"

Kevin stops dragging his chair.

Rain pummels the windows.

Teri glares at Megan then steps into the hall. "Nothing, Walter. Go back to sleep." She pushes Megan deep into the bathroom and closes the door.

Megan sets her jaw and speaks at normal volume. "A scout is going to be there."

"Two weeks. And keep your voice down."

Megan drops to a whisper. "Don't do this. Please."

"I warned you last time. Go to your room."

Walter bangs something against the door — probably a shoe. "Keep it down."

Teri keeps glaring at Megan. "You've brought this on yourself."

Megan clenches her fists then stomps to her room and slams the door.

Teri follows. "Three weeks!"

Lightning strobes through the windows.

The master bedroom door flies open and Walter, groggy and overweight, sways in black silk pyjamas. "What's the problem, now?" His black hair, still crusty with styling clay, is greying at the temples.

Thunder crashes overhead.

Teri turns to her husband. "I have it under control."

"Could have fooled me."

The lights flicker again.

In the kitchen, Kevin drops a bowl. It breaks.

Teri whirls. "Are you okay?'

Kevin pokes his head into the hallway. "I'll clean it up."

Walter snorts. "Bad enough with the storm and the boy breaking everything." He starts to close the door.

Teri turns back to her husband. "Walter, wait."

"What?"

"Would you please get Kevin after school?"

Walter closes the door.

Walter stumbles back to bed. Rain pulses against the window pane, muted by the drawn curtains. Crumpled clothing lies on the shag carpet and the room smells stale. Walter buries himself under the duvet.

Teri opens the door. "I'm trying my hardest here."

"And I'm not?"

"You're doing really well. I'm so proud of you."

Walter lifts his head.

"I've got a board meeting tonight."

"School, Library, or Health?"

"School. Kevin gets out at three."

"I've got a shoot." Walter pulls the duvet back over his face.

Megan's room is covered with hockey posters — mainly Team Canada but also the Toronto Furies and the Brampton Thunder from the Canadian Women's Hockey League. Her shelves are lined with trophies, medals, commemorative pucks, and team photographs — ten years' worth of collected accolades. Thunder shakes her shelves. Still in her towels, Megan transfers her gear from her drying rack to her equipment bag.

Teri throws the door open without knocking. "Walk Kevin home tonight."

Megan picks up her helmet. "Can't I be grounded tomorrow? You can double the time."

From the bedroom, Walter shouts. "Shut up!"

Teri closes her eyes for a moment then opens them again. She continues in a quieter tone. "Do as you're told."

Megan throws her helmet in her bag. "I hate you."

"Four weeks." Teri closes the door behind her as quietly as she can.

Teri checks her cell phone charging on the counter in the kitchen. No new messages.

Kevin, who's found another bowl, measures out the flour. "I can walk home by myself."

"Megan will meet you."

"I'm not a baby."

She pulls Kevin close. "No, you're the only person in this family who never lets me down." She kisses him on the head.

Half-an-hour later, Kevin waits by the open kitchen door. He's wearing his raincoat and rubber boots. His backpack is slung over his shoulder. Megan, who's now dressed in a clean hoodie, frayed jeans, and fresh running shoes, scribbles a note and leaves it on the table.

Teri starts the Prius and lowers the driver's window. The rain has almost stopped. "I'll be home around six."

Megan grabs Kevin's sleeve and drags him out of the house.

Kevin waves. "Bye, Mom."

Teri returns the wave and drives away, splashing through new puddles on the road.

Megan ducks back into the house then exits a moment later carrying two hockey sticks and her equipment bag. She hands the sticks to her brother and locks the door.

Kevin holds the sticks with both hands. "The national team! That's awesome."

Megan heaves her equipment bag over her shoulder. Bags with wheels are for little boys. "The national *Under-18* team. And only if the scout likes me."

"Everyone knows you're the best player in Dolsens."

Teri idles at the stoplight at Grand Avenue and Queen Street, rummaging through her purse. A murder of crows overflies the intersection heading south. They settle in the willows lining the Thames River. Still searching through her purse, Teri doesn't see the light turn green until the driver behind honks his horn.

Megan slips her cell phone from her hoodie pocket. "Dad will pick you up tonight, okay?" She punches in a brief text.

Kevin's smile fades a little. "Mom's going to freak."

"You know you're expected to rebel at some point."

Kim's grey Journey rounds the corner and pulls up to the curb, throbbing music.

Megan opens the back and throws in her equipment bag.

Kevin lays Megan's hockey sticks next to Kim's. "How come when you ask Dad to do something, he does it, but when Mom asks the same thing, he won't?"

"Vinegar doesn't catch flies."

Kevin frowns. "I don't get it."

"Neither does she."

Teri tiptoes into the kitchen. She finds her phone still connected to its charger. On her way to retrieve it, she spots Megan's note on the table.

Dad, NATIONAL scout @ game 2nite! Pls get Kevin. BTW found ur book.

Teri crumples the note and throws it in the garbage under the sink before writing a new note.

Walter, make sure Megan gets Kevin.

Gingerly, she steps outside and closes the door before opening her phone.

୨

The grey Journey pulls up to the curb at Clark Road Elementary School. As Kevin climbs out, Megan's phone rings. She checks the call display then returns it to her pocket, unanswered. Kim reminds Kevin not to forget his backpack.

୨

Teri leaves a voice message as she turns onto Queen Street. "I found your note, young lady. I am not impressed. If you don't pick up Kevin tonight, I will take you out of hockey for the rest of the season."

୨

Walter, barefoot but now dressed in black jeans and an untucked button-down shirt, rifles through the towel stack in the bathroom cupboard. He throws all the towels on the floor, then opens the other cupboard and then all the drawers. When he finally looks behind the toilet, he notices water has spilled down the tank, forming a small pool on the floor. He lifts the tank cover and finds *Intimate Photography*. He pulls it out and tries to wipe away the water damage, but it's no use. The book is ruined.

୨

Walter opens the fridge for the orange juice. He sets the towel-wrapped *Intimate Photography* on the table and sees Teri's note. He reads it as he drinks directly from the carton. After putting the juice back in the fridge, he erases the whiteboard and writes *294*.

⁓

Megan throws her books in her locker and slams the door. She checks the time on her phone. 2:30 PM. "Coming through!" Students cheer her on as they clear a path for her.

⁓

In his home studio off the kitchen, Walter loads a memory card into a digital camera. The towel-wrapped *Intimate Photography* rests on his desk. Framed black and white nude photographs line the walls.

⁓

Megan and Kim jog across the parking lot. The red and white team bus idles at the curb. Ashford Wilson, the team's manager, loads the mountain of hockey bags into the back. He's scrawny with a peach-fuzz moustache. The team has learned to post a sentry when they're in the showers.

Coach Paula Dillon, stands in the open doorway. "Ladd, Robbins, move your asses." She ticks Megan and Kim off her list.

⁓

Walter smiles at the nude woman crouched on his white paper backdrop. "Warm enough, Donna?" He lowers his camera.

The woman nods. Her chest is pressed against her legs while her forehead rests on her knees. "Is this how you want me?" She's in her early twenties and has a crescent moon tattooed on her left ankle. Her blonde hair fans across her back.

"Perfect." Walter raises his camera and snaps a shot.

The Dolsens School Board sits around a large table in the District Offices on Queen Street. Everyone wears dark, conservative suits. Lauren Jubenville, the recording secretary, is in her early twenties and is the youngest present. Jack Charron, who's in his sixties, is the oldest. It's been a long day.

Teri looks at the clock on the wall. It's just after 3:00 PM. "This decision is within our mandate."

Jack clears his throat. Both his jowls and his greying moustache quiver as he speaks. "George Sterling has been teaching in this community for over fifteen years. He has an exemplary record."

"He sexually abused a student."

Carol Anderson, the director of education, drums her fingers at the head of the table. Her makeup is perfect and her hair bun severe. She raises a finger. "Allegedly, Teri. George is still under investigation."

"So he gets to resign without charges?"

Jack puts his elbows on the table. "It's common practice."

Rob Bonner, another trustee who also happens to be a lawyer, nods. He's in his mid-thirties. His suit is Italian. His expression is a practiced neutral.

Teri leans forward. "We can't just let him walk away."

The sun shines through the maple trees and glistens on the dripping leaves outside Clark Road Elementary School. Still in his rubber boots, Kevin carries his raincoat in his arms. He's not wearing his backpack. While the other children disperse to sidewalks, the bike rack, waiting parents, or the line of yellow school buses, Kevin trudges to the curb and sits. A giant puddle spans the roadway — the storm drain is blocked with leaves and plastic wrappers.

⌇

Teri glances out a side window. A white sailboat heading upriver waits for the Queen Street Bridge to rise. "Shawn Giroux was the only boy brave enough to come forward. There may be others."

Jack drops his elbows. "Let the man resign with his pension intact."

"You should have declared your conflict of interest an hour ago."

"What conflict of interest? Are you saying I should abstain from this discussion simply because I live next door to George?"

"Possibly." Teri closes her eyes. "Yes."

"And shouldn't you abstain as well? Your husband — "

"What about Walter?"

"He's a pornographer."

Teri's eyes snap open. "He's an artist with a degree in photography from Ryerson!"

"Obviously, you condone sexually deviant behaviour."

"Do you want to step outside?"

Carol raps her fingertips on the table again. "Trustees, control yourselves."

Teri grips the table. "I want an apology."

"From me or your husband?" Jack sneers.

Rob shifts in his seat. "That's enough."

Teri stands. "Now."

Carol taps her fingers. "Mrs. Ladd, please."

Teri seethes. "I mean it."

After a nod from Rob, Jack inhales sharply. "Fine, in the interest of protocol, I apologize."

Teri sits and Carol asks if there are any other concerns regarding the allegations against George Sterling. While the other trustees return to the discussion, Teri spins her chair and calls Megan's number.

↬

Memorial Arena is packed with cheering students — red and white Matthew Dolsen Secondary School Loyalists benchside, green and white Dolsens Collegiate Institute Rangers concession-side. Plastic *vuvuzelas* drone. Beach balls bounce above spectators keeping a wave alive through its fourth rotation. Mist rises from the ice. The glass is fogging up. Coach Dillon paces along the bench.

At the faceoff dot, Megan scans the crowd. She smiles when she recognizes Barb King — an ex-Olympian — sitting with a clipboard behind the Loyalists' penalty box. Megan has a poster of King over her bed, the photo taken after the gold medal win at the Sochi Games. When the referee drops the puck, Megan slides forward and blocks the Rangers' centre. She slaps the puck to Kim on defence. As part of their set play, she does a quick up the ice and parks herself just short of the blue line.

↬

Kevin sits by himself on the curb. The yellow school buses close their doors and drive away.

↬

Teri looks at the clock again — 3:20. The sun reflecting off the river warms the room.

Rob leans forward. "We're not a judicial body. It's not for us to determine guilt."

Carol taps the table. "Agreed. Let the police sort it out. If George is innocent, we can apologize and reinstate him."

Jack rubs his face with his hands. "As long as we keep this quiet until the police make their report."

Carol sips a glass of water. "What do you say, Teri?"

"I can live with that."

Carol smiles. "Will someone make a motion?"

Teri calls Megan's phone again.

*

Megan dekes the defence and rushes the net.

The Rangers' goalie drops to her knees. Her face is red. Her ponytail is soaked. Her eyes are hard. "Bring it on, whore."

Megan fakes a shot and passes to Kim.

The goalie swears and repositions herself.

Kim slaps the puck back to Megan, who snipes it between the goalie's scrabbling legs.

The goalie sinks to the ice and hangs her head.

Megan leans down. "Tell your boyfriend I'm done with him, Five-Hole." She takes off her glove and lifts her jersey to display a pair of bloody men's underwear no one else can see. "You can have these back after the game." She lowers her jersey.

"Fuck you."

"*You* should fuck him sometime. We taught him a few things."

Rage

The goalie digs the puck out of the net and bats it down the ice.

Kim glides by. "Although he'll probably only want interracial FFM from now on."

"You want another black eye, bitch?"

Megan and Kim high-five each other and return to centre ice.

∽

Kevin watches two thirteen-year-old boys — Vince Laprise and Shawn Giroux — jaywalk across Clark Road in front of the nursing home. They're wearing faded jeans and army surplus combat jackets. Vince and Shawn graduated from Clark Road Elementary last year and now go to Megan's high school. Kevin retreats behind a large maple tree when he realizes they're heading his way. A black squirrel scolds him from the lower branches.

∽

The clock reads 3:25.

Carol taps the table again. "Did you get everyone's vote?"

Lauren nods as she types on her laptop.

"Motion carried. Next order of business?"

Lauren consults her notes. "The revised budget estimates."

Teri calls Walter's cell.

∽

Walter switches off his ringing cell phone and motions for a lean-muscled, nude twenty-something man to join Donna on the white backdrop. "Brent, let's start with a little spooning." Walter checks his lights and raises his camera.

∽

Vince reaches into his army jacket and pulls out a small firecracker. He lights the fuse and flings it at Kevin's tree. The firecracker explodes in mid air.

Kevin runs to the church on the other side of the road.

∽

Jack drones on. "The ministry requires all school boards to update their budget estimates based on the actual enrolment figures of October thirty-first." He pauses. "Am I boring you, Teri?"

Lauren stops typing. Rob raises an eyebrow.

Teri puts down her cell phone. "No, sorry. Please continue."

Jack clears his throat. "We've been directed to revise our budget to reflect grant enhancement allocations as part of the Provincial Table Discussion Agreements."

The clock on the wall reaches 3:30. Teri keeps her phone under the table and calls her home phone.

∽

Walter unplugs the ringing phone. He smiles at the nude couple and returns to his camera. "Shall we bring in our star?"

Donna and Brent get to their feet and approach a baby carrier. Donna coos. She lifts out their infant daughter, Fatima, and removes her sleeper. It's pink with bunny ears sewn into the thin hood. Brent drops the used diaper into the garbage can Walter holds out.

"Snuggle close to keep her warm." Walter puts a lid on the can and sets it down.

Donna and Brent hold their daughter between them and lie down.

Walter raises his camera.

Vince and Shawn laugh and duck behind the school.

Kevin stays beside the church.

⸙

Carol clasps her hands. "Do we have a motion?"

Rob raises his hand. "I move we receive the revised budget estimates report for the current year."

Teri raises her hand as well. "I second that."

When Carol asks if everyone is in favour, the vote is unanimous.

It's now 3:35.

⸙

Just into the Rangers' zone, Kim drops the puck for Megan, who charges forward and shoots hard on the fly.

The Rangers' goalie blocks the shot and swings her stick like a scythe at Megan's legs.

Megan twists away but trips over a coasting Kim.

Before Megan can get up, Kim circles back. "Don't retaliate." She nods at the note-taking scout.

Megan grunts, nods, and gets up.

⸙

From the sidewalk, Kevin watches the stray collie approach the school, sniffing at — and urinating on — random election signs and maple trees.

Vince and Shawn charge from behind the school. Vince lights another firecracker and throws it like a hand grenade.

The collie yelps and runs away.

⸙

3:40.

Carol takes another sip of water. "Moving along to the policy and regulations on home schooling."

Teri gets to her feet. "I'm sorry, but I have to go."

Rob makes a thin-lipped smile.

Jack leans forward. "Is everything all right?"

Teri gathers her belongings. "Not really, no." She runs out of the boardroom, calling home as she goes.

༄

As Donna and Brent get dressed, Walter cuddles Fatima, who's already back in her bunny suit with a fresh diaper. "I should have the proofs for you early next week."

Fatima pokes at his chin with her chubby fingers.

Brent smiles and tugs his pants on.

༄

Vince and Shawn lob firecrackers at a refurbished two-tone Ford F-150 pickup truck sluicing through the puddle in front of the school. The pickup swerves, spraying water over the sidewalk. Once clear of the puddle, the driver rolls down his window and curses.

Laughing, Vince and Shawn take off.

The pickup makes a U-turn and follows, honking its horn.

Kevin recrosses the road to sit on a dry patch of curb. He sighs, picks up some pebbles, and tosses them in the puddle.

༄

Teri speeds out of the district office parking lot in her Prius. She puts her cell phone on hands-free.

༄

Walter closes the door as Donna, Brent, and Fatima leave the studio. He plugs the home phone in and it rings immediately.

↬

Teri drives north on Queen Street, the traffic thickening near the Vintage Suites Hotel. "Don't hang up on me again."

"I was in the middle of a shoot."

"Tell me they weren't naked."

"We've been over this before."

Teri skids as a red Honda Civic suddenly brakes in front of her, the driver putting on his turn indicator only after he's stopped. "Your work makes me feel like a pervert."

The Civic makes its turn and Teri guns it forward, only to be stopped a block later by the rising Queen Street Bridge, its claxon wailing into the summer afternoon. Teri slams the wheel and looks to the river. The white sailboat she saw earlier is coming back. She turns off the engine. "Megan's not picking up."

↬

Walter opens the studio door and enters the kitchen. "Kids?" When they don't answer, he tells Teri they're not home.

↬

It's now 3:50. Teri grips the steering wheel. "I need you to get Kevin." Her knuckles turn white.

"It's only a couple of blocks. He can walk."

The bridge locks into its open position. "Grand Avenue is busy this time of day."

"You said Megan was getting him."

Teri's hands are starting to hurt. She releases the steering wheel. "Just tell me you're doing it. I can't hear anything else right now."

˷

After the second-period scrape, the Loyalists return to the ice. The school admins have confiscated the *vuvuzelas*, but the noise level is still deafening. The mist thickens. Kim skates behind Megan as they approach the bench. "Smile, show some teeth."

The scout nods when Megan looks up.

˷

Walter can't find his car keys. He's gone through the studio twice.

˷

3:55. Teri drums the steering wheel as the sailboat finally floats under the drawbridge. Dolsens needs another river crossing. One that's not a drawbridge.

˷

Miss Simpson, Kevin's grade five teacher, steps out of the school with earbuds in her ears. She's changed her nice shoes for sneakers but is still wearing her skirt and blouse. She takes her earbuds out. "Want me to wait with you again, sweetie?"

Kevin smiles and shakes his head. "No, thank you."

˷

Walter finally finds his keys in the front pocket of the pants he wore yesterday. On the bedroom floor.

˷

The sailboat clears the bridge. It's now 4:00. Teri restarts her engine.

～

Kevin watches Miss Simpson cross the street and walk the length of the nursing home.

～

The bridge is back down. The clock on the dashboard reads 4:05. Teri honks her horn to jump-start the drivers in front of her.

～

Walter races through Birdland in his Roadster. He rolls his eyes in the rear-view mirror. "I can't hear anything else right now."

～

At 4:10, Teri pulls up to the curb in front of Kevin's school.

Kevin jumps to his feet and opens the passenger door.

In the distance, two firecrackers explode. A dog barks.

"Maybe we should get you a cell phone."

Kevin climbs in. "Really? That would be awesome. Could I get some games, too? What about unlimited data?"

Teri mock frowns. "Then again, maybe not."

Kevin closes the door and mock pouts. "Oh." He clicks on his seatbelt. "How was your day?"

"The school board meeting was taking forever. Jack Charron is completely blind when it comes to . . ." Teri pauses. "You don't need to hear this. Where's your backpack?"

Kevin looks at his feet then pats his back.

"You can't forget your homework again."

Kevin unbuckles and throws open his door. "BRB!" He jumps out of the Prius.

"Pardon me?"

"Be right back! It's like a short cut, for texting! You know, on cell phones?"

Two more firecrackers explode. A dog yelps.

Teri leans over to close his door.

⌇

Walter turns onto Grand Avenue. Traffic is thick and sluggish. He pushes his foot down and changes lanes repeatedly.

⌇

Kevin bursts out the front door of the school, his feet slapping in his rubber boots. He holds up his backpack for Teri to see.

⌇

Walter turns onto Clark Road. He slows and is down to just ten over the limit by the time Kevin's school comes into view. The giant puddle glistens on the road. Walter spots Teri's Prius and swears.

⌇

Teri leans across the passenger seat to open the door for Kevin.

⌇

Vince and Shawn chase the collie down the sidewalk. Vince lights another firecracker. When it explodes on the collie's back, the dog darts across the road right in front of Walter.

⌇

Walter swerves and pumps his brakes. He misses the dog, but when his tires hit the giant puddle, they lose traction. His drive wheels whine and spin free. "Shit." Walter hydroplanes right for the Prius. He honks his horn. "Pull forward!"

⁓

Teri sees Walter heading right for her, spraying water in a titanic wave. "Kevin, get back!" She slams into reverse and stomps on the gas.

⁓

Walter spins his wheel to the right and when his wheels regain traction, the car jerks in response. But Teri's new trajectory keeps them on a collision course. "I said forward!" Walter grunts and spins the wheel hard to the left. He jumps the curb and passes in front of Teri's still-reversing Prius. Kevin is now directly in his path.

⁓

The end-game buzzer sounds and the Loyalists throw their helmets and gloves to the ice. Megan hugs Kim. The final score: Loyalists five, Rangers two. The scout nods. The red and white half of the crowd jumps the boards to swarm their team.

⁓

Walter stands on his brakes as he skids across the grass. "No!"
    Teri screams.
    Vince and Shawn run away.

298

TERI, MEGAN, AND WALTER, ALL dressed in black, sit in the first pew of Saint Richard's Anglican Church consciously not touching each other. Teri bites her lip. Megan has crossed her arms. Walter sobs. The church smells like lemon furniture polish and lilies. Kevin's coffin is draped in a white pall.

Scattered throughout the packed congregation are Lauren Jubenville, Jack Charron, Carol Anderson, Rob Bonner, and the rest of the school board. Coach Dillon sits with Megan's hockey team. Kim is with her father two rows behind Megan. Kevin's grade five class sits near the back with Miss Simpson.

The priest, a tired man in his early sixties, leads the service.

◡

Teri sits in the passenger seat of the funeral home's black Lincoln Town Car.

Walter, who's in the back with Megan, slips a mickey of rye from his pocket.

Teri shakes her head. "You'll regret it."

Walter considers the mickey, nods, lowers the window, and throws it out. The bottle smashes on the pavement.

Teri grips her purse. Her knuckles turn white.

Megan closes her eyes and sets her jaw.

Walter closes his window.

The Town Car follows the hearse at a crawl through downtown Dolsens. Crows roost in the willows by the river. Police officers salute from blockaded intersections. The procession crawls through every red light.

After five minutes of silence, Megan turns to her mother. "How about grounding for two months? No screens at all? No phone?"

"You're off the team for a year."

Tears slide down Walter's cheeks. "Isn't that a little harsh?"

Teri shakes her head.

Megan crosses her arms. "How was I supposed to know — "

"Want to make it forever?"

Megan clenches her fists.

Walter leans his head against his window. "Shit."

⁓

Kevin's coffin hangs over his open grave. Teri maintains her composure with difficulty. Megan stands to the side, her fists still clenched. Walter sobs again. The priest invites people back to the church's parish hall. Everyone offers lengthy condolences before returning to their cars.

Teri checks her watch. "Let's get the reception over with."

Walter wipes his eyes and follows Teri back to the Town Car.

Megan stares at Kevin's coffin. "Why'd you just stay there like a putz?"

⁓

Teri, dressed in a cotton nightgown, sits in bed, reading. Walter brushes his teeth in the bathroom. He finishes, enters the bedroom, and slips into bed.

The front door slams.

Teri sets her book in her lap. "All you had to do was make sure Megan picked him up."

Walter throws off the covers, grabs his pillow, and heads to the den.

⁓

Megan knocks on the front door of a red brick house on Dove Place. Solar garden lights line the walkway. The lawn is meticulously manicured. A slight breeze rustles the leaves in the ash tree.

Kim's father opens the door, a mixed drink in his hand. "Kevin was a wonderful boy."

"Is Kim home, Mr. Robbins?"

☙

Megan and Kim stumble down the sidewalk along Grand Avenue. It's now after 10:00 PM and the road is deserted. Streetlights bathe the night in yellow. Kim passes a bottle of gin to Megan who takes a long swig before passing it back.

☙

The gin is almost gone. The girls arrive at Kevin's school to find the collie sniffing at the grass where Kevin was killed. "Get away from there." Megan throws the bottle, hitting the stray on its shoulder.

The collie yelps and escapes behind the church.

Kim sits on the curb. "You can't be off the team."

"I won't be. There's no way I'm staying in this fucking town."

"How can I help?"

Megan shrugs. "At the moment? Get me laid."

"Want to double team Hoekstra again?"

Megan shakes her head. "Find me something new."

☙

By 11:00, Megan and Kim have crossed the Thames River and are passing the Myrrh Tree Motel. Just beyond the motel, country music leaks out of the McCrae House. They walk through the parking lot and climb the front steps.

A bouncer with a long moustache and no body fat stops them. He's wearing a blue jacket with brass buttons, trimmed with a high red collar and yellow sergeant's stripes. He must be in his late twenties. "Hold it right there, ladies." Dolsens is just big enough to not know everyone.

Megan looks the bouncer up and down. "What's the problem?"

"Got any ID?"

Megan bats her eyes and whispers, "Fuck me."

The bouncer puts his ear close to Megan. "What was that?"

Kim taps him on his bicep and hands over two I.D. cards.

"Christine Chapel and Janice Rand?" He laughs and returns the cards.

Kim throws out her boobs. "Those are our real names."

"So does that make me Kirk, Spock, or McCoy?"

Kim glances at Megan. "What are you talking about?"

"I guess I would be more like Chekov, after he got promoted to chief of security."

Kim stamps her foot. "Those IDs are good."

Megan shrugs.

"Go home." The bouncer points to the parking lot. "And don't come back until you're old enough to stop smelling like pee."

Megan clutches his sleeve. "I really want you to fuck me."

299

Walter, still in his black pyjamas, enters the kitchen to find Teri dressed in a blue skirt suit and pouring muesli into a bowl. The whiteboard on the fridge reads *298*. Walter turns to the table and sees it's set for four. He starts to take a place setting away.

Teri abandons her breakfast, grabs her purse, and leaves the house.

Walter watches her drive away. The front end of his Roadster is scraped and slightly caved-in. He pours a bowl of muesli for Megan, erases the whiteboard and writes *299*, then starts to cry as he makes his way to his studio.

∽

Megan enters the empty kitchen. She takes the bowl of dry muesli from the table and throws it in the garbage without tasting it.

∽

Still crying, Walter connects his digital camera to his computer. Halfway through uploading the photographs of Donna, Brent, and Fatima, he stops, unplugs the camera and throws it on the floor. The outer casing cracks.

∽

Teri's parked outside Kevin's school, watching the children at recess. The storm drain has been cleared and the puddle has dried up. The bell rings and everyone rushes inside.

∽

Megan sits in class staring out the window.

Mr. Turner, her socials teacher, turns from the chalkboard. "Miss Robbins, what do you think?"

Kim looks at Megan, but doesn't get a response. "I think I didn't do my homework."

The class laughs.

Kim looks at Megan again.

This time, she smiles weakly.

Mr. Turner addresses the class. "Can anyone tell me why the family is the primary agent of socialization in Canadian society? Anyone? Please, tell me at least one of you did the reading."

Megan shrugs and returns to the window.

⸻

Sobbing, Walter looks at pictures of Kevin on his computer: the day he was born, being pushed by Megan in his stroller, his first steps, sitting in his high chair, his first bike. Walter's camera lies on the floor.

⸻

Teri is still outside the school when the dismissal bell rings. The yard swells with children. School buses fill quickly. Jack Charron drives out of the parking lot and pulls up next to Teri. He rolls down his window. "I am so sorry."

She closes her eyes.

"Would you like a cup of coffee?"

Teri shakes her head.

"Why don't you skip the meeting today? I promise not to let George Sterling off the hook until you're back to fight me on it."

Teri opens her eyes but doesn't say anything.

Jack rolls up his window and drives away.

⌇

Megan runs through her practice drills faster, harder, and with at least three more degrees of skill than anyone on her team.

The scout watches from the stands and scribbles notes on her clipboard.

⌇

Still sobbing, Walter prints out picture after colour picture of Kevin.

⌇

Back at home, Megan slams the door of the nearly empty refrigerator. People have finally stopped leaving casseroles on the doorstep. Her hair is wet from a recent shower. Through the window, she watches Teri pull into the driveway and enter the house. "What's for dinner?"

Teri sets her purse on the counter.

Megan rolls her eyes. "You're not speaking to me now?"

Teri walks the length of the hallway and closes her bedroom door without saying a word.

Megan opens her mother's purse and takes out a credit card. She grabs the house phone and dials a number. "Give me two large meat-lover's. With a six-pack of Coke, breadsticks, ribs, and a double order of chicken wings."

⌇

Walter sorts the pictures of Kevin on his studio floor. He's placed his broken camera on his desk.

Megan enters, carrying a pizza and a can of Coke. "Dinner." She points to the picture of her pushing Kevin in a stroller, her skates tucked into the storage rack underneath. "I remember that day. I pushed him all the way to the arena."

"Why didn't you pick him up?"

Megan's eyes snap up. "I left you a note."

༄

Megan reaches into the kitchen garbage under the sink, pushing aside chicken bones, the rib container, and dry muesli until she finds the crumpled note. She puts it in her back pocket.

༄

Megan knocks on Teri's closed bedroom door. She's carrying two slices of pizza on a plate and a can of Coke. "Mom?"

Teri doesn't answer.

"I've got dinner."

Teri still doesn't answer.

"I'll just leave it here." Megan sets the food on the floor. Before straightening, she shakes the can."

༄

Teri lies alone in bed, staring at, but not reading, her book.

༄

Megan and Kim sit cross legged on the front lawn of Kevin's School and share another bottle of gin. Streetlights bathe the night in yellow and the cicadas buzz from the willows near the river. The air smells like yeast from the ethanol plant. The collie walks by.

Megan jumps up. "You just keep on going."

Startled by her sudden movement, the collie shies and runs away.

Kim checks her watch then stands, too. "I'd better get going."

Megan nods. "Leave me the bottle."

⤴

Walter channel surfs in the den. His eyes widen as Megan enters and sets the remaining gin on the coffee table. "Get rid of that."

Megan takes the crumpled note from her pocket and hands it to her father. "Mom threw it away."

"Why didn't you tell me about the scout?"

"Why'd you leave your shit book in the bathroom?"

Walter's cheeks redden. "You trashed it."

"We agreed that was over."

"Your mom came home early last Tuesday and I panicked."

"Fuck, Dad, I brush my teeth in that room. Find somewhere else to jack off."

⤴

The pizza and Coke sit untouched outside the master bedroom door. Megan spits on the pizza.

⤴

Teri lies alone in bed, staring at the ceiling. Her book, still unread, sits in her lap. She flinches when Megan slams her bedroom door.

⤴

Walter considers the gin bottle for a full hour before he finally picks it up and finishes it.

300

THE SUN CRESTS THE HORIZON to a cloudless sky. Starlings chirp and flit between the ash trees. Dew steams off the sidewalks. Teri delivers newspapers, dressed in her ball cap and running crops. At a house on Pheasant Drive, she stops when she sees the nameplate over the mailbox. Sterling. Teri slips the bag — still filled with papers — from her shoulder and leaves it on the doorstep.

∽

Walter makes coffee. He's wearing his black jeans and a black T-shirt. Pizza boxes rest on the counter.

Megan enters the kitchen, dressed for school in cut-off shorts and a button-down blouse.

Walter, his eyes red-rimmed, takes a coffee cup from the cupboard.

Megan sees the pizza boxes then looks in the garbage. She removes the empty gin bottle, glances at her father, then puts it back under the rib container. She crosses to the whiteboard and replaces the *299* with *300*.

Before Walter can say anything, Teri enters the kitchen without speaking to either of them and goes down the hallway.

∽

In class, Megan stares out the window.

Vince and Shawn saunter up the walkway to enter the school.

Megan checks the time. 9:30.

∽

Walter places the photos of Kevin in a leather photo album.

∽

Teri, still dressed in her running crops, sits in her Prius outside Kevin's school. The collie walks down the sidewalk, sniffing at maple trees, fire hydrants, and election signs.

∽

At Memorial Arena, Megan and Kim leave the ice after practice.

The scout waits near the dressing room. "Megan? Got a minute?"

∽

Walter waits by the kitchen window, watching Teri park in the driveway. Two paper bags filled with take-out sushi sit on the table, along with the photo album.

Teri enters the house and goes straight to the bedroom.

Walter picks up the photo album and follows.

∽

Megan pushes open the kitchen door with a huge smile on her face and her hockey bag over her shoulder. She looks down the hall and sees Walter standing in the bedroom doorway.

Walter closes the door behind him.

Megan tiptoes to her room and slides her hockey bag inside, then knocks on her parents' door.

Walter opens the door. "Shh."

Megan grins. "Guess what?"

"Not now." He closes the bedroom door again.

Megan knocks a second time. "Dad?"

Through the door, Walter says, "Shit, just wait."

༄

Megan stomps down the hall into the kitchen. She opens the sushi containers and spits in all of them. She looks back down the hall.

The master bedroom door is still closed.

She shoots her finger at it, then notices the open bathroom door. She goes in, grabs the laxatives from the medicine cabinet, and returns to the kitchen.

Her parents still haven't come out.

Megan crushes a handful of pills under a can and sprinkles the powder over the sushi, then puts the containers back into their bags.

༄

Teri cries on the bed looking at the photo album.

Walter sits beside her. "Please, say something."

She closes the photo album.

Tears spill down his cheeks. "I didn't mean to do it."

Teri points at the door and turns back to the photo album. "Get away from me."

Walter slams the bedroom door and hurries through the hallway. As he enters the kitchen, Megan hides the laxative bottle behind her back. He starts to sob.

Megan rolls her eyes. "Now can I tell you my news?"

"Can't it wait?" He makes for his studio.

She clenches her fists. "Don't forget your dinner."

Walter grabs one of the sushi bags and goes to his studio.

⁌

Two hours later, Teri is still on her bed, flipping through the photo album. Her cheeks are tear streaked and used tissues cover the floor like crumpled snow.

⁌

Walter scrolls through photos of Teri on his computer, slouched in his swivel chair. Their wedding day. Their honeymoon in France. The day Megan was born. The remains of his sushi — mainly the ginger and wasabi — sit on his desk. A pained expression crosses his face.

⁌

Teri examines a picture of her with Kevin and Megan. In the photo, Teri and Kevin hug twelve-year-old Megan in a towel at the beach. The four of them had gone to Rondeau Park on Lake Erie for a picnic, and Megan had gotten her first period while swimming. Six-year-old Kevin had given her a towel so she could get back to the car without anyone else noticing. Walter had started drinking shortly after. Teri stares at the photo until she reaches out to touch her children's faces.

⁌

Rage

Walter sits on the toilet clutching his stomach. His face is pale and his hair is streaked with sweat.

∽

Teri leaves the bedroom clutching the photo album to her chest. She enters Megan's room. The light is off. "Megs?" When she doesn't get an answer, Teri turns on the light.

The room is empty.

Teri is about to leave when she sees Megan's hockey gear on the drying rack. She touches first her chest protector, then her elbow pads, then her shin pads. They're all damp.

∽

Teri marches out of Megan's room and stops in front of the bathroom. "Megan?"

Walter groans from inside. "It's me."

She pounds on the door. "We need to talk."

"Oh God, please, just go away."

∽

Teri storms into the kitchen and grabs her cell phone. She scrolls through her contact list and calls Megan's coach. "This is Teri Ladd. Megan is off the team."

Coach Dillon asks if there's any way Mrs. Ladd will reconsider. Megan needs all the training she can get to prepare for her first tournament with the national Under-18 team.

"My decision is final." Teri hangs up and sets her phone down. She throws the remaining sushi bag into the garbage.

∽

On the toilet, Walter clutches his stomach. His face is pale. "Teri?"

Teri stomps down the hallway. "What?"

"I don't feel so good."

"Deal with it." She slams the bedroom door.

⌒

Megan and Kim sit on the bouncer's jeep in the McCrae House parking lot. The streetlights are just coming on. Faint stars scatter across the darkening sky. The wind ripples through the willow branches.

The bouncer exits the bar and takes off his jacket. "You girls want a ride or something?"

Megan smiles at Kim. "You up for a little FFM, Janice?"

⌒

Teri sits at the kitchen table. Crickets chirp outside. On the table is the photo album of Kevin. It's 3:30 AM.

Megan opens the door. She smells like sex.

"I called your coach."

Megan clenches her fists.

The toilet flushes in the bathroom, and Walter enters the kitchen, rubbing his eyes. He's still pale. "What's going on?"

Megan folds her arms across her chest. "I made the national Under-18 team."

Walter's eyes widen. "Yeah?"

Teri closes the photo album. "You're out of hockey."

Megan drops her arms to her sides. "Don't do this."

Walter faces Teri. "No!"

Teri pushes her chair back from the table. "Kevin is dead!"

Megan steps back. "That's not my fault!"

Teri stands. "You ditched him!"

"You are such a fucking hypocrite."

Walter raises his hands in supplication. "Everyone just calm down."

"You were supposed to walk him home!"

Megan rolls her eyes. "Kevin was cool with it."

Teri glares. "And now he's dead."

Walter turns to Teri. "Megan didn't kill Kevin."

Teri slams the table. "You both did!"

Megan's mouth drops open. "What?"

Walter paces in a circle and throws his hands in the air. "I need a drink."

Teri points to the *300* on the whiteboard. "Go ahead, it's your solution to everything."

Walter's face collapses.

Teri picks up the photo album and marches to the hallway.

Walter calls after her. "This is your fault as much as ours."

Megan nods. "It so fucking is."

Teri clutches the photo album tighter to her chest. "You killed my son!" Tears cascade down her cheeks.

Walter's eyes flare. He punches a cupboard and wood splinters fly everywhere. "It's all I think about!"

"Well think about it some more!"

Megan sets her jaw. "We found the note, mom."

Teri turns around. "What are you talking about?"

"The note I wrote Dad, asking him to get Kevin. You hid it on purpose."

"If you'd just answer your goddamn cell phone, I wouldn't have needed a note."

"Maybe I wasn't ignoring you. Maybe my phone was just off. You ever think of that?"

Teri's eyes harden. She returns to the kitchen and holds out her free hand. "Give it to me."

"What?"

"Give me your goddamn cell phone."

"You going to check my call history?"

"Now!" Teri snaps her fingers.

Megan shrugs and hands Teri her cell phone.

Teri smashes it on the floor. "There, that can't happen again!"

Megan bends to pick up the pieces of her phone. "You're fucking mental."

"Stop swearing around me, goddamn it." Teri stamps her foot.

Megan scoops up her phone and stands. "Why don't you fucking bite me?"

Teri clenches her fists. "You are on such thin ice, Megan."

Walter's eyes widen. "Teri, calm down."

Megan brings her face within a handspan of her mother's and enunciates slowly. "Fuck you." She snatches the photo album from Teri's arms and throws it against the table. The album's spine breaks and photos fly everywhere.

Teri's face turns white. "Go to your room!"

Megan turns to Walter.

He looks at the ruined album and bends to gather the scattered photos. "Do it. If you'd just walked him home, none of this would have happened."

301

Walter finds Donna's deposit cheque in his files and stuffs it in an envelope. As he looks for a stamp to return her money, he sees his *Intimate Photography* book wrapped in the towel. He sits back and flips through the ruined pages, each containing a single black and white photograph he took. All are nudes. Walter opens the curtains to let in some natural light.

Walter unsticks a page and laughs. A dark-skinned couple balance on their buttocks, hands clasped, their touching feet forming an inverted "V". Walter couldn't believe some of the tantric poses they'd asked him to record. Both were yoga instructors, and were incredibly fit. And flexible.

Another few pages on and he finds an older couple pressing noses.

The next page shows a young couple looking up from the backdrop paper. Walter had climbed a ladder to get the effect he wanted, both of them cradling her pregnant belly.

Walter closes the book and looks at his broken camera on his desk. He gives up on the stamp and takes out the memory card.

∽

Megan sits in socials class staring out the window. Starlings flit along the gravel parking lot.

Mr. Turner clears his throat and taps the blackboard with a piece of chalk. "Care to join the rest of us, Miss Ladd?"

Megan starts to roll her eyes until she sees Vince Laprise and Shawn Giroux saunter up to the school doors. Vince shows a handful of firecrackers to Shawn, who nods and smiles. Megan checks the time: 9:30.

∽

Teri is parked in front of Kevin's school again, wearing a summer-weight sweater over her crops. A dozen white roses lie on the passenger seat. She watches as the caretaker cuts the grass with a blue tractor, not even pausing as he crosses the spot where Kevin died.

∽

As Megan puts on her shin pads in the Loyalists' change room, Coach Dillon pops her head around the door. "Ladd, out here."

Megan follows.

"I've been told you're off the team."

Megan sets her jaw. "That's not fair."

"Without your mom's consent, there's nothing I can do. I'm sorry."

Megan clenches a fist. "This is bullshit."

"Don't get mad at me."

"What am I supposed to do now?"

"Make up with your mom? I need you."

"Fuck." As her now former coach returns to the change room, Megan punches the boards. The glass wobbles halfway around the rink.

∽

Teri lays the roses on the churned earth of Kevin's grave.

∽

Megan trudges through Birdland, lugging her hockey bag. When she reaches one of her mother's election signs, she crosses the grass to kick it. The sign wobbles. Megan kicks it again. And again. And again until the post breaks and it finally falls.

⥲

Teri pushes an empty grocery cart through the supermarket. As she passes the deli counter, Carol Anderson accepts a wrapped package from the clerk and calls out. "Teri. Good to see you."

Teri stops her cart.

Carol puts on a smile. "You would have been proud of Jack Charron, yesterday. George Sterling has really been pressuring him, but Jack is refusing to let him get away with it. He's now recommending a suspension."

Teri stares at Carol until the older woman smiles awkwardly and excuses herself.

⥲

Megan and Kim watch a bootleg Kontinental Hockey League game and drink Mr. Robbins' gin in Kim's darkened basement. Magnitogorsk leads Lev Praha, seven to four. Megan mutes the volume. "Want to go see Ed?"

Kim sips some gin. "Not really."

"How come?"

Kim passes the bottle to Megan. "Honestly?"

Megan takes a drink.

Kim scrunches up her nose. "Your bouncer's breath smells." She shrugs. "Sorry."

⥲

Walter adjusts the hue and saturation levels of the photos of Donna, Brent, and Fatima on his computer. Through the open window, he notices Teri pull in the driveway.

Teri locks the Prius and approaches the house. She sees Walter looking at her through the window.

Walter waves, tentatively. As he powers down his computer and turns out the studio lights, Teri enters the house.

Outside the McCrae House, Megan pulls away as Ed the bouncer leans in to kiss her. "Not tonight."
 "Why not?"
 Megan rolls her eyes. "I'm on the rag."
 "Oh."
 Megan shrugs. "There's something I've got to do, anyway."
 Ed steps back.
 "Want to help?"

Walter makes dinner — a ratatouille recipe they'd discovered in a Monoprix on their honeymoon. As he sautés an eggplant, Teri nibbles a wedge of Brie on a sliced baguette. It's not as soft as the banettes they had in Paris, but the bakery selection in Dolsens is rather limited. Walter has set the table for three.

Rage

As Ed's jeep idles next to the curb, Megan approaches one of Teri's election signs and tries to pull it out. It won't budge.

Ed leans out the window. "Do you need to use those signs again?"

"No. Why?"

Ed goes to the back of his jeep and grabs a tire iron. He hits the post and it breaks easily.

Megan picks up the fallen sign and throws it in the jeep.

Ed hands her the tire iron. "You might work for this Ladd lady, but I don't." He climbs back behind the wheel.

"You got a threesome last night."

Ed turns off the engine. "How many more signs, Christine?"

"All of Birdland."

∽

An hour later, Teri and Walter eat their dinner alone. She sets her fork down. "Did Megan say anything to you?"

"Do you want me to have a talk with her?"

"She's supposed to be grounded."

∽

Megan and Ed take Teri's election signs from the back of the jeep and throw them in a dumpster behind the Myrrh Tree Motel.

∽

Walter washes the dishes as Teri looks out the kitchen window. "I'm calling Kim." She reaches for her cell phone.

Walter shakes his head. "Megan's got a lot to process right now."

Teri returns to the sink and picks up a tea towel. "Fine."

∽

Megan gets out of Ed's jeep at the Birdland entrance — the corner of Grand Avenue and Crane Drive. "Later."

∽

Teri enters the living room in her nightgown as Walter tucks blankets on the couch. "You want to come to bed?"

"I'd like to." He searches Teri's eyes. "Does this mean?"

"One step at a time."

"I can accept that." He follows her into the bedroom.

Teri slips under the covers and picks up her book.

o

MEGAN AND KIM HAVE SKIPPED socials class to wait for Vince and Shawn. Both girls wear denim miniskirts and tight-fitting tanktops. When the boys arrive at 9:30, Megan, who is taller than both of them, walks straight to Vince and punches him in the face. "You know why, don't you?"

Vince swallows and nods. Blood pumps from his nose. He makes no move to defend himself.

A very short, very one-sided fight ensues. Kim holds Shawn, making sure he can neither help Vince nor run away.

∽

Dressed in her blue skirt suit, Teri drives to the District Offices to discuss George Sterling's now-documented harassment of Jack Charron. She's almost out of Birdland before she realizes all of her campaign signs are missing. And only her signs. Teri parks and marches up to a sign reading *Re-Elect Jack Charron, a Trustee You Can Trust!* Next to it, a shattered post sits where one of her signs used to be.

The next yard over, the collie sniffs one of Rob Bonner's signs and lifts its leg.

Teri whistles and approaches the dog, her hand open. "Come here."

The collie tucks its tails between its legs and bolts.

Teri gives chase.

⁌

A pimple-scarred and mulletted clerk cradles Walter's broken camera in his hands. "It's going to be cheaper to buy a new one, Mr. Ladd."

Walter shakes his head. "I thought so."

The clerk sets the camera down. "What do you want to do?"

Walter points at an expensive model under glass. "I'll need some good photo paper, too."

⁌

Vince lies on the ground in the foetal position. His face is bloody. Students line the windows of the school.

Megan turns to Shawn. "Your turn."

Kim holds him from behind, just above his elbows. "Take it like a man."

"I'm sorry. Oh crap, I'm so sorry."

Megan punches him in the mouth. "Just shut the fuck up."

Blood courses from Shawn's lips. Tears fall from his eyes. Snot drips from his nose. A tooth falls out. "I didn't mean to hurt your brother."

Kim puts her knee into Shawn's back. "Vince never whined."

Eventually, Mr. Turner arrives and drags Megan and Kim away. He turns to the students in the windows. "Get the school nurse."

～

The collie squirms under a backyard fence.

Teri stops to catch her breath. Her cell phone rings. The call display reads Matthew Dolsen Secondary School. Teri turns her phone off.

～

Walter and Megan exit the high school together. Her knuckles are split and bloody again. Behind them, Kim is being dragged away by her father. Vince and Shawn have already gone to the hospital. A police cruiser sits at the curb, but both boys swore the fight was consensual. Walter opens the passenger door for his daughter. "You want a milkshake?"

"How about something stronger?"

～

Teri knocks on a front door. The name Quigley is spelled out in brass letters above the mailbox. A tall, slim woman with a white ponytail and a pressed brown pantsuit answers.

"You shouldn't let your dog run loose."

The woman lights a cigarette. "Pardon me?"

"Your dog caused an accident."

The woman shakes her head. "I don't have a dog, dearie."

"My son was killed."

The woman blows smoke to the side. "They shed all over the place."

"I saw it crawl under your fence."

The woman looks outside. "My sister used to keep cats."

Rage

※

Walter and Megan sit on the couch watching a retrospective on Terry Sawchuk. A half-empty bottle of rye sits between them.

※

Teri peers over Mrs. Quigley's backyard fence. She can't see anything but trimmed grass and rose beds.

※

Tears course down Walter's cheeks. The empty rye bottle rests in his lap. "Shit."

Megan kisses Walter on the forehead.

※

Teri opens the gate to Mrs. Quigley's backyard.

※

Megan's lips brush Walter's.

He shakes his head.

She covers his lips with a finger. "It's okay."

Walter sinks his head back into the upholstery of the couch.

Megan grabs her father's wrists and leans forward. She kisses him again.

A sob contorts Walter's face.

※

Teri finds a second hole on the far side of the yard. She strides across the grass and climbs over the fence. She catches her nylons on a loose nail.

※

Walter pulls back. "I promised not to."

Megan presses herself against him. "Vinegar."

"What?"

She kisses him again then sets the rye bottle on the floor. "For old time's sake." She pulls down her underwear then unzips his pants.

Walter covers himself as she tugs off his jeans. "No."

Megan hikes up her skirt and straddles her father's lap. "Put this on." She slides a condom from her back pocket.

Tears course down his cheeks. His hands are shaking. "Are you sure?" He drops the condom.

She sets her jaw and picks up the condom.

∽

The collie lifts its leg on the base of a child's backyard swing set.

Teri's heels sink into the ground. Sweat stains her jacket. "Come here, you stupid mutt."

The collie cowers. Its fur is matted and burnt in patches. Blood drips from fresh wounds around its ears.

She holds out her hand.

This time, the collie lowers its head and licks her fingers.

Teri knows she's going to take it to the vet.

∽

Walter scooches to the far side of the couch. Tears streak his face.

Megan pulls her skirt down and steps into her underwear. "Give it to me."

"What?"

She rolls her eyes. "The condom."

∽

Teri enters the kitchen and sets her purse on the counter. She takes off her suit jacket and drapes it over a chair. Then, she kicks off her shoes and rolls down her ruined nylons. After putting them in the garbage, she opens the fridge for the orange juice. She tries to pour herself a glass, but can't because the carton is empty.

Megan enters with the empty rye bottle. She throws the condom in the garbage and places the bottle on the counter. "You look like shit."

"Why aren't you in school?"

"Bite me."

Teri points at the bottle. "Where did you get that?"

Megan shrugs. "Dad bought it."

"No."

"Yup." Megan skips to the whiteboard and erases *301*. She replaces it with *0*.

"Have you been drinking?"

"Yup."

Teri points at Megan's freshly-split knuckles. "And fighting again?"

Megan rolls her eyes. "You noticed. I'm touched."

Walter stumbles into the kitchen. He shakes his head when he sees the rye bottle.

Megan smiles at her mother.

Teri's hands fly to her hips. "Go to your room."

"Not this time."

Teri turns to Walter.

His fly is undone and there's a wet stain at his crotch.

Megan smirks.

Teri's hands fly to her face. "What did you do?"

Megan rolls her eyes. "As if you don't know."

Teri steps forward and slaps Megan across the face. "You little bitch!"

Megan mouth drops open, but only for a second. She makes a fist and punches her mother full force in the face.

Teri falls against the table and crashes to the ground.

Megan stands over her. "It went on for three years. You had to have known."

Blood spurts from Teri's nose. "What are you talking about?"

Walter steps back toward his studio.

Megan spits on her mother then grabs Walter's hand and leads him out of the house.

〜

Teri clambers to her feet. Blood from her nose stains her silk blouse. She runs cold water in the sink. Through the window, she sees Walter's Roadster back down the driveway with Megan behind the wheel. Teri grabs the rye bottle and smashes it in the sink.

〜

Megan takes Walter to the Myrrh Tree Motel. Dusk is coming on. She parks in front of reception and holds out her hand. "Got your credit card?"

He stares at his feet.

She turns off the engine and pockets the keys. "Give me your wallet."

〜

Teri calls Walter's cell.

〜

Megan leads Walter to room 104 and closes the door behind them. It's musty and smells of stale cigarettes. She tugs off Walter's jeans.

He doesn't try to stop her. "Again?"

She bundles her father's jeans into a ball. "Later."

༄

Teri marches into Walter's studio and finds his cell phone ringing on his desk. She hurls it against the wall. The proofs of Donna, Brent, and Fatima are laid out on his desk. Teri picks them up to destroy them and finds the water-ruined copy of *Intimate Photography* underneath. Walter had it published last year. Teri starts to flip through. Black and white nudes splash across every page. Women, men, couples, families — all nude. When she gets to page forty-six, Teri drops the book and collapses to the floor. It's a nude shot of Megan, her back arched, her eyes closed, draped across Teri's bed. It looks like it was taken two years ago — about the same time Teri's significant community service had been recognized with the Queen Elizabeth II Diamond Jubilee Medal.

༄

Walter, naked, sits alone on the bed watching television. It's tuned to the local cable channel broadcasting a rerun of the Loyalists–Rangers game.

Megan opens the minibar and collects all the little bottles. She lines them up in front of her father.

He doesn't respond.

"I'll be back."

༄

Teri grabs a box of garbage bags and heads to the master bedroom where she strips the sheets from the bed.

⁓

Walter opens the first bottle and drinks it down. It's rum. When it's gone, he reaches for a second. Scotch.

⁓

Teri stuffs Walter's clothes into garbage bags — everything from the discards on the floor to the remaining T-shirts in his dresser to the dirty pants in the hamper. As twilight settles outside, rain starts to patter on the roof.

⁓

Megan enters the McCrae House. A few patrons catcall, but Ed shuts them up with a glance. Twangy country music pumps from hidden speakers. Sawdust covers the floor. A replica Brown Bess is bolted to the wall, as well as a portrait of Tecumseh and a pair of crossed flags — a Union Jack and a Star-Spangled Banner.

Ed intercepts her at the bar. "You can't come in here."

Megan considers the bartender — a scowling twenty-something woman with multiple tattoos and piercings wearing a feathered stovepipe hat — and turns to Ed. "I need a favour."

"What?"

Megan caresses Ed's left bicep. "Gin."

Ed ushers her to an empty corner.

"My period's over."

Ed frowns.

She takes Walter's wallet from her pocket, grabs a handful of bills, and puts them in his hand. "Maybe I'll bring Janice with me."

Teri drags an overstuffed garbage bag into the kitchen and leaves it next to the three full bags already there.

～

Megan pushes her father onto the mattress and opens the first of two large bottles of gin.

His eyes are red.

Rain taps the window glass.

～

In the kitchen, Teri finds Megan's shoes coated with dried mud. She puts them in a garbage bag.

～

Megan straddles her naked father. Her skirt rides over her hips, but this time she's wearing underwear. "You know why I'm doing this, don't you?" She opens the second large bottle.

"I don't want anymore."

"I'm your daughter, you fucking pervert."

～

Teri throws Megan's things into garbage bags — her trophies, her clothes, her hockey gear, her posters, her bedding. Thunder rumbles.

～

Megan pushes the bottle of gin passed her father's teeth. He can't help but drink.

～

Teri stacks garbage bags around the wheeled bin at the curb. The street lamps glisten in the hammering rain. Over-stretched plastic rips open. Underwear and socks strew across the lawn.

∽

Megan climbs off Walter's inert form. She rolls the empty gin bottles onto the floor and puts her ear to his face. She hears nothing.

∽

Teri sits on the front step, staring at the mess of clothes strewn over the lawn. Mist rises from the grass. Rain straggles her hair. She leans back and looks to the clouds.

∽

Megan picks up the hotel phone.

∽

Teri's cell rings in the kitchen. She shrugs and continues to look up. If anything, the rain is getting heavier.

∽

Megan gets in the Roadster and starts the engine. Ed's tire iron rests on the passenger seat.

The Edmore Snyders

I find *Southwestern Ontario Archaeology for Dummies* on my cleaning station when I return from the washroom. My fists clench. Paul has made a fake cover and taped it to a site report. I throw the mock guide in the garbage, stuff my hands in my skirt pockets, and count down my days — *quatre, trois, deux, un*. I refuse to let the little passive-aggressive wiseass provoke me, so as usual, I suppress and deflect. I force my hands open and pitch my voice with ersatz cheerfulness, "*Très drôle*, Paul. Very funny."

There's a creak on the stairs, a stifled chuckle, and the back door closes.

Counting down is the only effective calming technique I've got. I've used it through my criminal conviction, my six month incarceration at the Vanier Centre for Women, and the three years of my parole. In four more days — *quatre jours* — I report to my parole supervisor for the last time. Then, I get my life back.

I take a deep breath and pick up where I left off, washing chipping detritus — the stone flakes left over from the manufacture of prehistoric lithic tools — essentially cast-off litter. They're from the Benscoter Site. *Quatre jours*. Counting down has gotten me through this demeaning job, my pay-by-the-week apartment, the ostracizing grimaces of former colleagues, and the time I'm losing from my research. *Ma recherche.* I always count down when I have to clean chert flakes for James D. Gulliver, BA, licensed principal of Heritage Resource Consultants, an archaeological salvage company out of London, Ontario. Jim pays me minimum wage, but he's not sexist. He pays his other year-round staff member, Paul Hallam — the little passive-aggressive wiseass — the same as me. And, Jim gave me a job in archaeology when no one else would: not the museum, the university, the Ministry of Transportation, or any other salvage company in the city. He even promised a supportive reference letter for when I'm finished my parole.

I dip a frazzled toothbrush into a plastic tub of muddy water. No matter how often I empty the tub, it still smells of decayed organic matter. I grab the last flake and scrub it clean. Paul says the Benscoter flakes are important technological remnants of a people gone for over six hundred years. I say who ever heard of a consequential archaeological find made in suburban Ontario? Everything here leads to nothing.

My fists are clenching again. *Quatre, trois, deux, un.* Let me start again. My name is Stacey Dunlop and I'm thirty-four years old. I have a master's degree in European palaeolithic archaeology from the University of Toronto. I love savoury *crêpes salées* and delicate Pinot Noirs. I drop the flake onto my cleaned pile and check my tally against the collection form. Twenty-six. I blot everything dry with a paper towel and ink sequential catalogue numbers onto anything larger than my thumbnail.

I should have a PhD in European palaeolithic archaeology. I should also have my own protected site in the Dordogne Valley in France, where I should be unlocking the secrets of the early cave painters with the help of generous private and academic grants. But I don't and I'm not. Instead, I'm atrophying in this desolate Canadian hinterland because I let a different passive-aggressive wiseass ruin my life. Alain Bédoier is the reason I don't have my own crew of eager volunteers and experienced grad students. He's the reason I'm not doing real archaeology. He's the reason I'm only practicing my French instead of speaking it full time. A little over five years ago, Alain seduced me with his clipped accent, his enthusiasm for European prehistory, and his ability to cook crêpes, all while stealing substantial portions of my dissertation. If I hadn't been forced to rephotograph the figures at Font de Gaume after my original shots disappeared, the Doctoral Advisory Committee might have believed me instead of Alain. As it was, he presented first, I was last, and they didn't. When I saw my original photographs published under Alain's name, the police ended up taking him to the hospital and arresting me.

Quatre jours.

I complete my portion of the collection form. Paul says the flakes are Onondaga chert. I'll have to take his word for it. He specializes in Great Lakes' cultures and is Jim's field director. Paul says the Benscoter Site was a seasonal hunting camp overlooking the Thames River near my home town of Dolsens. Whatever. All I know is these flakes are dark grey with some inclusions of partially silicified limestone. I'm a European specialist. I don't have time for this backyard shit.

Before I can open the nail polish to smudge-proof the numbers, Jim asks me to come upstairs. The lab is in the basement of a dilapidated heritage house Jim bought when he started the company. His office is on the main floor, in what used to be the dining room, and smells of discount instant coffee. Jim offers me a steaming enamel mug emblazoned with *have trowel, will travel.*

"Stacey, I'd like you to take the artifacts from the Edmore Site to the museum." Jim slurps from his own mug — *archaeologists do it in the dirt.* He's about forty-five and his greying hair needs trimming. Badly. There are two drip strains on his chest. I suspect he's still a virgin.

"I'm cataloguing Paul's lithics."

Jim sets his mug on his desk. "Ken convinced Charles Edmore to donate the entire collection." Charles Edmore must be the landowner. Ken is Dr. Kenneth Weldon, the director of the local Museum of Prehistoric Archaeology. "I'd like you to do it before lunch."

"*Certainement. Pas de problème.*"

Jim's phone rings and he picks it up, effectively dismissing me.

I check my watch and take my coffee downstairs. 10:15. I pass my cleaning station and the reconstruction table where the remains of an Iroquoian cooking pot I've been reassembling sits. The pot is also from the Benscoter Site and is nowhere near as old as my 17,000-year-old cave paintings. At the back of the lab, Paul's desk is buried under a pile of site reports, archaeological society newsletters, academic journals, and a brochure for a resort along the Côte d'Azur. I toss the brochure in the garbage and sift through the rest of the clutter until I find the key to the storage room. Paul and I share a set.

The storage room used to be a root cellar and smells like petrified mouse droppings. I flick on the florescent lights. Floor-to-ceiling aluminum shelves hold hundreds of liquor boxes filled with artifacts, stored in trust by Jim for their rightful owners. In Ontario, the law says everything found on an archaeological site belongs to the landowner, but let's be honest — who could possibly want a box of broken pottery and chipped stone? The boxes are labelled with magic marker and masking tape.

I find the Edmore Collection among some vodka boxes near the back wall. I carry the collection through the lab and set it on the vacant table between the Iroquoian pot and my cleaning station. I don't remember working on Edmore, but the handwriting on the box is definitely mine. It's from three years ago.

I take out the collection form to make sure I've got everything. I don't want to give Jim a reason to give me anything less than a glowing reference. Edmore should include twenty Snyders projectile points, all intact and made from Upper Mercer chert — whatever that is. There should also be three spokeshaves, four bifaces, a T-drill, some potsherds, a handful of chipping detritus, and some fire-cracked rock.

I check the T-drill and the potsherds. The T-drill looks like something I might find in France: a cylindrical cone made of black chert with a wide, flat base. It would have been used for drilling holes in leather, wood, or bone. *Très bien.* The broken pottery looks like it was decorated by pressing a cord into wet clay. *C'est bon.* The spokeshaves are made from black chert with blue and white bands, as are the bifaces and all of the chipping detritus. *Bon, aussi.* Like their European counterparts, spokeshaves were used to make arrow shafts. Bifaces were sometimes used as knives. Fire-cracked rock has been deliberately heated, usually for cooking.

Next, I lay out the projectile points on the table, and frown. I don't know what a Snyders point is supposed to look like, and honestly I don't care, but these points aren't all the same type and they don't feel like flaked stone at all. Some are spear points, others only arrowheads, and none of them are crafted from the black chert with the blue and white bands I can only assume is Upper Mercer. Most are yellow, two are red, and one is grey. On closer inspection, I see the material they're made from is porous, with a silica temper — it's got to be fired clay. No European culture made ceramic projectile points because they would have shattered on impact and I've got to assume native North Americans wouldn't have, either. Paul must be messing with me again. *Merde.*

"Stacey!" It's Jim calling from the dining room.

I grab my coffee and climb the stairs.

Jim drums his fingers against his empty mug. "What's keeping you?"

I check my watch: 11:00. "It's not lunchtime." I take his mug and bring it to the kitchen where I surreptitiously dump mine.

Jim follows me, grabbing a knotted tie from the coat tree by the back door. "I said before lunch. The museum closes early on Fridays." Little blotches of red appear on his cheeks.

I rinse both our mugs in the sink and decide not to add to Jim's stress by revealing Paul's latest practical joke with the switched points. "I'm still looking for the artifacts."

Jim slips his tie over his head. It's blue with silver stripes. "Vodka box, near the back." He tightens the knot with shaky fingers.

"D'accord."

"I'll be at a meeting downtown until one." Jim pulls on his jacket, a brown tweed with suede elbow patches. "Make sure the complete collection is delivered before I get back."

I nod and place the mugs on the drying rack.

"Or you're fired." He slams the door on his way out.

My fists clench. I have no idea where Jim's ultimatum came from, but I can't lose my only job reference now. I'd been hoping to apply for the new study of Grotte de Cussac next week. *Quatre jours.* I've lost my patience for Paul. I stomp out the back door.

⁓

I find the little passive-aggressive wiseass in the equipment shed behind the work van — a decommissioned Hydro vehicle Jim bought at auction. The equipment shed used to be a carriage house. Paul has the swing doors propped open with a wheelbarrow and is listening to some *yé-yé* punk on a mud-splattered CD player. It might be just in my mind, but to me the shed still smells faintly of horses.

Jim's rusted two-tone station wagon pulls out of the driveway and turns left on Lyle Street, heading downtown.

I try to ignore the French music as I step into the shed. "Where are the points, Paul?"

Paul Hallam is a graduate student in his mid-twenties with a shaggy beard and a stringy ponytail. He's sitting on an overturned bucket, repairing the screens we use to sift dirt. He wears a jean jacket, cargo shorts over ripped long johns, and steel-toed boots. Paul joined the company two years ago. "Read any good guidebooks lately?" He smiles.

I stoneface him. "From the Edmore Site."

Paul shrugs and trims excess wire mesh from a roll. "You look in the storage room?"

"I'm not in the mood."

Paul sets his wire cutters on the ground. "The box should be labelled."

I step closer.

Paul slides back. His bucket scrapes along the concrete.

"Joke's over." I grab the little passive-aggressive wiseass' jacket and lift him to his feet. His bucket tips and rolls away.

Paul's eyes widen. "You've only got four days left."

Quatre, trois, deux, un. A second assault conviction will destroy everything. I let him go. "Those points have to go to the museum today."

Paul picks up the roll of wire mesh and holds it between us. "What are you talking about?" I swear he smirks a little.

"You switched out the Edmore points!" My fists clench and I punch the roll. It spins out of his hands.

Paul retreats behind the screens. "I never tamper with artifacts."

I kick his CD player, sending it tumbling across the floor. The music stops when the cord pops from the outlet.

Paul circles to the open door, keeping the screens between us. "I'm the one who thinks Ontario prehistory is worth something, remember?"

I count down again. *Quatre, trois, deux, un.* He looks terrified with his palms up and his shoulders cringing. Could he be telling the truth? I take a deep breath and try to recall every prank he's ever pulled: tying my boots together when I'm asleep in the van, writing archaeological word-of-the-day definitions in crayon on my lunch bag, spray-painting my trowel orange, cocooning my canteen in caution tape, the *Southwestern Ontario Archaeology for Dummies* this morning. He's never once tampered with an artifact. I unclench my fists and jam my hands into my skirt pockets. "I'm sorry."

Paul bites his lip.

Inside my pocket, I find a loose thread and roll it between my thumb and forefinger. "I don't know what the points look like."

Paul lowers his hands. "What type?"

"Snyders."

Paul sets the CD player upright but doesn't plug it in. "Ace of spades."

"Really?"

"Snyders points were made from an ovate preform, have round corner notches, long barbed shoulders, and usually have a straight basal edge. They look like an ace of spades and are between fifty-five and seventy-five millimetres long." Paul picks up the wire cutters and puts them in a toolbox. "They date from 200 B.C. to A.D. 50. Early to mid-Hopewellian."

The description I understand. The culture reference, I haven't got a clue. "The points in the Edmore box aren't Snyders. There's supposed to be twenty of them."

"A cache?" Paul looks instantly earnest.

"I didn't read the site report."

"This I've got to see." Paul leads me out of the shed, like a preschooler chasing down an ice cream truck.

⌒

Paul straightens from where I'd laid out the Edmore points. "They're fakes."

"No shit."

Paul picks up a small yellow arrowhead with side notches and a wide triangular base. "It looks machine moulded. See the seam?" I swear he smirks again.

I slap the table. "Where are the fucking points, Paul?" Artifacts bounce in the air.

Paul returns the collection to the box, leaving the fake points on the table. "I can't wait until you're back in France!" Paul dodges my cleaning station, sprints up the stairs, and slams the door.

"This is bullshit!" I slap the table again. "*C'est des conneries!*" A fake point falls to the floor and cracks in two.

⌒

I look in Paul's desk, opening every drawer. I find pens, pencils, callipers, more newsletters and journals, and another French brochure, but no projectile points. I try for rationality. Paul respects this backyard shit, so he's probably stashed the points where they won't get damaged. I throw out the brochure and grab the storage room key. The other vodka boxes are all empty. The next closest hiding spot is the Soper Site in a gin box. The collection form is filled out in my handwriting. When I find a point, my fists clench. It's a yellow ceramic fake. *Merde!*

The next five boxes — all processed by me — have had their projectile points replaced with ceramic replicas. *Quatre, trois, oh putain!* This is more than a practical joke, Paul has set me up. Not only will I be fired, I'll be accused of stealing the originals. Jim will never give me a reference now.

I open boxes at random. A rum box, the second in a series of seven from the Scotford Site, shows me how far Paul has gone. It's from a Neutral village he excavated last year. Not only are the original points missing, but the box was supposed to contain a ceramic effigy pipe shaped like a fox. The pipe is gone. In its place are broken potsherds. *Je suis baisé.*

I go to the very back of the storage room and dig out the hardest-to-access box I can find. It's a tequila box holding the Russell Site, a thousand-year old ceremonial burial overlooking the Grand River. Jim excavated it ten years ago, long before Paul or I had joined the company. The original points have been replaced with ceramic replicas. *Merde! Merde! Merde!* More than likely there isn't a single original projectile point left. There's no need to keep up my French practice any longer. I'm fucked. Paul has won. Like the Doctoral Advisory Committee four years ago, Jim won't believe I'm innocent. I check my watch: 12:30. I've got half an hour. I pocket a fake point and run upstairs.

The carriage house's swing doors are still open. High-pitched and off-key French singing fills the air.

Four, three, two, one. I force myself to walk the last few steps around the van. I stuff my hands in my pockets, cupping my right hand around the fake point.

Paul is eating a sandwich on his bucket. "What do you want?" He stops chewing. "Actually, cancel that. I don't care."

I eject the CD from the player and throw it over the van like a Frisbee. "Tell me where you hid everything."

Paul swallows a mouthful of sandwich. "I told you before, I never tamper with artifacts."

"The Soper Site?"

Paul just sits there.

"The effigy pipe from the Scotford Site?"

"What?"

"Replaced with broken potsherds."

Paul drops his sandwich. Bread and lettuce and tomato tumble onto the concrete.

I step closer, but he looks more stunned than smug or self-satisfied. He's not even cowering. Maybe he didn't do this. I take a deep breath and try another tactic. I take the fake point from my pocket. "Where could you get something like this?" I throw it to him.

Paul tenses and catches the fake with both hands. "No pressure flaking scars. It hasn't been knapped."

"I didn't ask you to analyze it. I asked where you could get one." My fists clench and unclench.

"The museum gift shop or that recreated Iroquoian village on Highway 2."

I pitch my voice gently. "Paul, tell me the truth. Is this another prank?"

"Stacey, I'm looking forward to next Tuesday as much as you are." He swallows.

"You really didn't do this?"

"Absolutely not." Paul shakes his head and stands. "What are we going to do?'

"We?"

"If all of those points are missing, it means someone has stolen them. Think of the lost history. We need to find the thief and recover the artifacts."

I clench my fists, but release them when Paul steps back. "I don't care who took them. If I don't deliver twenty Snyders points to the museum in..." I check my watch. "...twenty-five minutes, I lose Jim's reference and my shot at France."

Paul returns the fake. "Any chance the artifacts just got mixed in with another site?"

"Every box I checked had their originals swapped out with fakes. This is intentional." I put the fake back in my pocket. "Would the museum or the recreated village sell real points?"

Paul shakes his head. "Only replicas. A local collector is your only chance."

I nod. At five dollars a point I could replace the whole collection for one hundred dollars. "Know anyone?"

Paul picks up the pieces of his sandwich. "We could check the Internet."

We go inside and sit down at Jim's computer. It's a ten-year-old desktop running outdated software. The keyboard is slimed with coffee stains and crumbs. Paul throws his ruined sandwich in the garbage. We search for locals selling native artifacts, and before long, find a shop downtown advertising twenty Snyders points. A wave of hope warms me. I click through to the shop's website and bring up their list of Snyders points. The page takes forever to load because Jim doesn't have high speed. Finally, it comes up. The Snyders are beautiful. Some are so thin they're translucent, glowing in the backlight they were photographed with. Paul was right, the good ones look exactly like an ace of spades. And then I see the prices and my hopes crash like a dropped ceramic. The cheapest point is fifty dollars. The most expensive, seven hundred fifty. Most of them are in the two hundred dollar range. This theft is bigger than I thought. I won't just be losing a reference — I'll be arrested. "I had no idea people paid this much for arrowheads."

Paul stands. "Can you afford it?"

I shake my head. "There must be thousands of dollars of artifacts missing downstairs."

"Without a provenance, those artifacts are worthless."

My mind starts to wander, trying to find a motive. "Maybe it was a summer undergrad trying to supplement Jim's minimum wage?"

"One way to find out." Paul heads down to the storage room. "The Talmage Site."

I follow. Talmage was an Archaic lithic scatter from Thornhill I processed last week, after the undergrads returned to class. It's in a brandy box. We open it and sift through the plastic baggies until we find the points. The originals — which Paul says were supposed to be Nettlings — are gone.

Paul reseals the Talmage box. "It's got to be Jim."

I get a sinking feeling in my chest but try to ignore it. "No way."

"Who else could it be?" He points at the aluminum shelves. "How many times has someone asked to see these? My guess would be Edmore is the first."

When I first started here, Jim would take me out to dinner every Friday. Even brought me flowers on my birthday.

Paul paces in a circle. "He'll lose his licence."

Jim had hired me under a government make-work scheme for ex-cons, paying half my wages while the government covered the rest. I clench my fists and refocus on Paul. "With my criminal record, I'm a perfect scapegoat." At the time, I thought he was doing me a favour: the work wasn't European, it wasn't research, but at least it was a chance to stay in archaeology.

"But what does he do with the money? Everything he owns is an outdated piece of crap."

This feels just like Alain's betrayal. I've been so focused on not reacting to Paul's torments I forgot to protect myself from Jim.

Paul crosses his arms. "I'll quit."

I stuff my hands in my pockets. "If Jim thought far enough to hire me as a patsy, he'll implicate you, too." At worst I'd feared Jim had an unreciprocated crush.

Paul bites his lip.

I check my watch. 12:50. Once I'm in prison, the past four years of washing chipping detritus won't seem so bad. I'll probably even miss Paul's practical jokes; this morning's *Southwestern Ontario Archaeology for Dummies* was a well-crafted imitation, much better than the potsherds Jim replaced the Scotford effigy pipe with. I smile. "What about replacing the missing points with chert flakes?"

"What kind of chert were the Edmore points?"

I think back. "Upper Mercer."

"That's black, with occasional blue and white striations." Paul thinks for a second then opens a whisky box and reaches inside. He pulls out a plastic baggie filled with black chipping detritus.

⁓

Paul and I find enough Upper Mercer flakes from other sites to serve as convincing broken Snyders points, choosing only flakes too small for catalogue numbers. Paul makes a note of where we took each flake from, so we can replace them later. Any reconstruction will reveal our subterfuge, but I'm hoping Dr. Weldon won't accept the collection when he sees the damage. We reseal the baggies, tape the box closed, then load the modified Edmore Collection in the van. I check my watch. 1:15. Jim could return any second. Paul climbs in the driver's seat.

"What are you doing?"

Paul buckles up his seatbelt. "Going with you."

I shake my head. "Jim will get suspicious."

"We share keys, remember?" He starts the engine.

I get in. "Thanks."

Paul puts the van in gear and turns left onto Lyle Street. "I think that's the first time I've ever heard you say that."

My fists clench, but I relax them. He is saving my ass, after all.

⁓

Paul stops at the red light at York Street, three cars back. We need to turn left.

I check my watch. 1:20.

Traffic backs up into the intersection while we wait for the light. Only two cars get through.

"We don't have time for this." My fists clench and unclench. "King Street is faster."

Paul grips the steering wheel. "We're blocked in."

I check my mirror. A brown delivery truck is right behind us, practically touching our bumper. I can't stuff my hands in my pockets because of the seatbelt, so I fold my arms across my chest.

When the light changes, the car in front of us creeps into the intersection. The driver is too timid.

I honk the van's horn. "Keep going!"

Paul pushes my hands away from the wheel. "Stacey, chill."

I glare at him. "Drive around."

"I can't."

The car in front of us completes the turn after the light turns red. I fume and wait for the light to change again. Traffic builds and the intersection almost clears, but just as the opposing light turns yellow, a silver SUV guns it and stops in the middle of the intersection, cutting us off completely.

I reach over and lean on the horn.

Paul pushes my hand away.

The SUV driver looks at me, then impassively raises his middle finger.

My fists clench and rage fills my chest.

The SUV driver keeps a completely expressionless face. He's not angry or laughing or even remorseful. Nothing. He just keeps his middle finger in the air. And then he smirks a little, just like Alain did at my sentencing.

I reach for the door handle.

Paul touches my arm. "Stacey, don't."

I flick Paul's hand away. "He's completely in the wrong and he doesn't give a shit."

"I know. But if you get out of the van, you'll be charged, not him."

I roll down my window. "Get out of the way!"

The SUV driver keeps his finger up.

I'm so angry, my vision starts to tunnel.

Paul grabs my arm. "Calm down."

I glare at him, seething. "Piss off."

Paul winces but doesn't back down. "Don't give him the power to fuck up your life."

My teeth grind. My heart pounds in my chest.

"Focus."

I try counting down — four, three, two, one, four, three, two, one — but it doesn't work in English. The language just reminds me of what I'm losing. And that reminder makes things clear. I will not give up my last chance to salvage my 17,000-year-old cave paintings for some passive-aggressive asshole in an SUV who probably can't even spell the word archaeology. Or an artifact thief who's never been laid. I take a deep breath from my gut. Two, three times. "Okay." I unclench my fists.

Paul cranes his neck forward. "You sure?"

I take another deep breath and nod. Four, three, two, one. "Yes." I do my best to look anywhere but at the SUV driver: the delivery truck behind us, the westbound traffic moving normally, the car rental lot across the road. My heart doubles a beat — Jim's rusted two-tone station wagon is in the lot, parked next to a building with blacked-out windows.

Paul smirks. "This is his downtown meeting? No wonder he's late."

My rage diffuses with uncertainty. "Renting a car?"

Paul shakes his head. "Look closer."

The cars in the lot are all a little dusty, as if the lot closed a month ago. The building with the blacked-out windows looks abandoned, but has a neon open sign glowing in the glass door. Over the door is a larger sign, painted black on white: *Luxury Girls Erotic Massage.*

"So that's where his money goes." My fists clench again.

The lights change and the silver SUV clears the intersection. Paul oversmiles and gives an insincere wave. I refuse to look so I don't know what the SUV driver's reaction was.

While we wait for the next green, Jim exits the massage parlour. He blinks until he gets his sunglasses on, then walks to his station wagon, digging the keys out of his pocket.

The light changes and Paul enters the intersection. We still can't turn with the traffic so thick on York. There must be an accident.

Jim gets in his car, starts it, and drives to the edge of the rental lot. His face hardens when he sees us.

I touch Paul's arm lightly, making sure my hand is open. "Find another route."

Paul nods and spins the wheel, doing a three-point turn. He floors the gas pedal.

The Museum of Prehistoric Archaeology is landscaped low to the ground and is topped with a replica Iroquoian palisade. A man leans against a red vintage convertible near the entrance wearing a black sweater, jeans, and suede cowboy boots. He's in his late fifties and sports a white-streaked goatee. I recognize him from Paul's archaeological society newsletters.

Paul parks to the right of the convertible, Jim on the left. The rest of the parking lot is empty.

"Dr. Weldon," I say, stepping out of the van. The air smells of sun-bleached pine.

He extends his hand. "Stacey Dunlop, I've heard you do good work."

I shake his hand. It's warm to the touch. And dry.

"Hello, Paul," Dr. Weldon says.

"Ken." Paul comes up behind me.

Jim climbs out of his station wagon and approaches from Weldon's other side. "Where's the Edmore Collection, Stacey?" Red blotches bloom on his cheeks.

I smile and point behind me. "In the van."

Jim glances at Dr. Weldon but speaks to me. "I told you to have them here before lunch. You've kept Ken waiting."

Maybe Dr. Weldon is Jim's partner is this. My hands tremble as I keep them from clenching.

Jim stares me right in the eye. "Did you open the box?"

My rage rises. Four, three, two, one. I will not give him the power to ruin my life. "Yes."

Jim's left eye twitches.

Paul smiles at Dr. Weldon. "The Edmore Snyders are amazing specimens."

"Have you seen them before?" I ask.

Dr. Weldon shakes his head. "Just pictures from the site report." No one without a theatre background could affect the kind of anticipation he's presenting — forward-hunched shoulders, an unguarded smile, and sparkling eyes. Dr. Weldon has to be innocent.

Jim's hands are shaking. "Have you seen the points, Stacey?"

I jam my own hands deep into in my pockets and cup the fake point. Four, three, two, one. Alain never got in my face the way Jim is doing, he just hung back aloof like the SUV driver. Staying clam is incredibly hard, but I will not let my anger show. Four, three, two, one. I nod. "They're gorgeous. So thin, almost translucent. I've never seen such exquisite craftsmanship. Just like twenty aces of spades." I realize as I'm laying it on I actually believe it. The projectile points on the website — while not in the same league as my cave paintings — are amazing in their own right. I take the fake from my pocket and give it to Jim. "I believe this is yours."

Jim jams the fake in his jacket pocket, out of sight.

Dr. Weldon steps forward. "What is it?"

Before Jim can answer, Paul shifts his weight behind me. "Stacey, the Edmore Collection?"

Refocused, Dr. Weldon smiles. "Yes, please."

I open the side door as non-aggressively as I can. I slide the Edmore box toward me and slit the taped lid with my nail. I can do this. As I raise the cardboard flaps, I pretend to slip on the loose gravel. I fall and take the box with me. The box hits the ground first, and with a slight twist, I manage to land on top of it, crushing the cardboard. "Oh my God."

Paul kneels to help me. "You okay?"

I'm going to have bruises. "The Snyders."

Jim's mouth drops open.

Paul helps me up.

Dr. Weldon lifts the crushed box to the hood of his convertible.

I reach inside and pull out one of the projectile point baggies. I simulate horror as best as I can. "They've shattered."

Dr. Weldon looks crestfallen.

"That's impossible." Jim's cheeks quiver. "There's no way your little fall could have done this kind of damage." Jim reaches into the box and pulls out another baggie. "I should fire you right now."

"I'm so sorry," I say. The itch to hit Jim is breath stealing. Four, three, two, one. Four, three, two, one. Four, three, two, one. "Maybe I got the wrong box. Let's go back to the storage room and check the others."

Jim pales. "You bitch." His voice trembles.

Paul steps forward. "Take it easy, Jim. *Stacey* didn't do this on purpose."

Jim glares at Paul.

Paul smiles. "Besides, she has only four days left."

"What?"

I nod. "And one more meeting with my parole supervisor."

Paul takes the baggie from Jim and puts it back in the box. "You know she has to report everything that happens to her."

Jim clenches his fists.

"And then I'm off to France for good." I get my hands back in my pockets and let Jim make the next move. For the first time in a long while, I feel empowered, not exploited, but I know that could change in a second. It all depends on Jim's reaction.

Jim looks from me to Paul and back again.

Dr. Weldon dumps the contents of the box onto the hood of his convertible. "They're broken! All of them." Chert-filled plastic baggies spill everywhere.

I pull at my loose thread and say nothing.

Spit forms at the corner of Dr. Weldon's lips. "This can't be happening."

I keep my eyes on Jim. "Will you still give me that reference?" I keep my hands in my pockets. "I'd like to part as friends."

Eventually, Jim nods, then steers Dr. Weldon toward the station wagon. "Ken, it looks like this just wasn't meant to be. Let me buy you a beer. We can cry over this together."

Dr. Weldon's face reddens as he walks away. "Twenty Snyders gone. Twenty!"

Paul and I collect the baggies from Weldon's convertible and put them in the van. As I close the door, I exhale slowly, and smile. Only four more days. *Quatre jours plus.* Paul slips into the driver's seat and starts the engine. I climb in beside him and together we drive away.

A Flock of Crows is Called a Murder

1703 hours, 21 February 1951 (Wednesday)

GARY WEARS MY WINTER BOOTS from last year as he stands sentry under the catalpa tree in the front yard, the BB gun with the magnifying scope cradled in his arms. I keep tabs from the porch, standing easy with the range-finding binoculars. A warm breeze from the west field brings the scents of thawing dirt, rotting corncobs, and last year's cow manure. Yesterday's rain has dissolved the snow into ankle-deep puddles, so I'm wearing Mom's lace-up flight boots in case I'm needed for a sortie.

Gary sights south across Fourth Line to Dolsens Airfield where Dad's new black and chrome Cadillac Sixty Special advances along the access road. Behind him, Mr. Thane pushes his single-engine high wing into the civilian hangar. It's a Cessna 120, just like Mom used to fly, although Mr. Thane's Cessna doesn't have the optional electrical system. His 120 is only authorized for day operations. Gary lowers his weapon. "All clear, Louise."

Our homework is finished. A tuna casserole is in the oven. The mail — an uncancelled French fashion magazine, a bill from Sterling's Department Store, a letter for Dad with an American stamp from the US Department of the Air Force, and today's *Dolsens Daily News* — is sorted and waiting on the foyer table. I'm about to give Gary the thumbs-up when a crow overflies our house and glides the length of our property to touch down in the shallow ditch along Fourth Line. Its black feathers flash blue in the dying sunlight.

Gary swears and clicks his cocking lever seven times, dropping a BB in the chamber.

I bite my lip and check the binoculars. Fifteen yards. "Out of range."

Gary fires anyway. His BB whiffs into the grass, five yards short.

The crow ignores him and pecks at a rancid corncob floating in the ditch.

Gary reloads, advances three paces, and fires again. Another undershot.

At the end of the access road, Dad's Sixty Special turns on to Fourth Line. His tires crunch gravel.

The crow raises its head and zeroes in on the sound. It caws three times in quick succession — staccato bursts like a sten gun.

The hair follicles on my neck stand up. Our encyclopaedia calls it horripilation.

Gary presses forward and fires a third time. His BB overshoots and skips along the road.

The crow bunches its shoulders, extends its wings, and takes off, setting an intercept course with Dad.

I charge off the porch and sprint across the yard, waving my arms in large circles. My feet slide side-to-side in Mom's still-too-large boots.

The crow spots me and aborts its attack. It swoops across the road to perch on the nearest scarecrow — one of five empty flight suits Dad's cadets nailed to wooden frames last fall.

Gary yells at me to clear his sight line and fires again. His BB grazes the crow's tail feathers.

The crow squawks and leaps into the air, beating its wings hard. It pulls a steep climbing turn to gain altitude just as Dad's Sixty Special reaches the farthest scarecrow.

I grab a handful of pebbles from the road and hurl them at the crow. I don't even come close. They fall like wasted shrapnel.

Dad brakes hard and his tires skid. His bumper pitches back and forth.

I bend for another handful of pebbles, but before I can throw them, Dad leans into the horn. Startled, I jump to the left. My feet slip on the wet grass and I slide into the ditch. Mom's boots fill with frigid ankle-deep water. I raise the binoculars overhead to keep them dry.

The crow circles one last time then retreats toward the setting sun.

Dad releases the horn and powers down his window. He stares at us briefly, then closes his eyes like he's done for the past five months whenever something should upset him.

Gary comes trotting up. "All clear."

I consult my wristwatch. "Tuna casserole will be ready in twelve minutes, sir."

Dad opens his eyes, powers his window up, and drives into the carport. By the time Gary helps me out of the ditch and we return to the house, Dad is in the foyer reading the letter with the American stamp. Gary races into the kitchen.

"Leave the casserole alone!" Gary knows his only pre-dinner assignment is setting the table, but sometimes he expands his operations without briefing me. I place the binoculars on the foyer table. "Everything in order, sir?"

Dad slips the letter back into its envelope, turns toward his study, and speaks to me over his shoulder. "I've been assigned to the US Air Force's Fourth Fighter Interceptor Wing at Kimpo."

"But you're in the Royal Canadian Air Force." I straighten and clasp my hands behind my back.

"Exchange duty. Fifty Sabre missions or six months, whichever comes first." Without facing me, Dad retrieves his tobacco pouch and pipe from his pocket then holds out his greatcoat. "Look after your brother while I'm gone."

"Yes, sir." I take his greatcoat and hang it in the closet.

Dad fills his pipe with tobacco, steps into his study, and strikes a match. Smoke puffs into the hall as he closes the door.

I unlace Mom's boots and pull them off. My bobby socks stick inside and my feet come out pink and wrinkled. I leave the boots on the rubber mat and grab the rest of the mail. When I get to the kitchen, Gary waits in his chair, swinging his legs — he's only nine and still can't reach the floor. I set the mail on the counter by the phone and grab the oven mitts. While I take the tuna casserole from the oven, I brief Gary on Dad's orders.

Gary regards his empty plate and his shoulders slump. "I know you can do it, Louise. I mean you're thirteen and you already do all the cooking and you're the one who washes the clothes, and you're the one who wakes me up for school."

I set the casserole on the table. "But?"

"How will we get groceries?"

"You know the milkman comes Tuesdays and Thursdays." I check the kettle on the stove. The water is starting to boil.

"He doesn't have cookies, Louise. Or bacon."

I drop a spoonful of instant coffee into Dad's cup. "Or tuna or noodles or frozen peas." I look around the kitchen. On the counter, the bill from Sterling's Department Store catches my eye. Dad orders things on account almost every month — aftershave, shoe polish, civilian underwear. "Maybe Sterling's can deliver."

"Their cookies are crummy."

"Got any better ideas?" I fill Dad's cup with hot water.

Gary shakes his head.

We hush as Dad enters the kitchen, places his pipe in the ash tray, and sits down. He takes a deep breath and closes his eyes again.

I spoon casserole onto our plates, take my seat, and say grace.

Gary separates the peas from his tuna and noodles. "F-86 Sabres are way better than Hurricanes or Spitfires."

Dad opens his eyes to sip his coffee.

Gary spears a chunk of tuna. "But the new MiGs have a really high ceiling."

Dad sets his cup down and offers a slight smile with his head down.

I take a bite of casserole. It's mostly cooked through. "Sabres are faster at low altitudes." We've always discussed comparative aircraft specifications and aeronautical manoeuvres at the table. When Mom hadn't been racing on the women's circuit, she'd been a civilian instructor with Dad's cadet squadron. She used to take us flying on weekends, patiently showing us how best to use the rudder pedals and control wheel.

"Just get them before they climb." Gary demonstrates — his fork becomes an F-86, his spoon a MiG. He weaves them back and forth over his plate until the F-86 cuts off and shoots down the spoon. It crashes into his peas.

I wipe my mouth with a serviette. "Is there anything we can help you with before you ship out, sir? I'll pack your kit bag, of course."

Dad blackens his noodles with pepper. "Help your Aunt Sylvia." He still hasn't looked either of us in the eye.

"You called her from the study."

Gary finds another pea and sets it aside.

"She'll be here next Thursday." Dad reaches for the ketchup.

When everyone has left the table, I do the dishes then add the fashion magazine to the box under my bed. We haven't seen Aunt Sylvia since Mom's funeral.

1506 hours, 1 March 1951 (Thursday)

THE MERCURY HAS FALLEN BELOW thirty and the ground is once again buried under thick snow. While the other kids race off school property to throw snowballs until the school buses open their doors, I slow march to Dad's idling Sixty Special at the curb. My overcoat is too small to button up. I'm wearing my red saddle shoes with the pink cardigan Mom gave me two Christmases ago. Gary runs ahead to claim the front seat. He's got black Oxfords and his green bow tie. He can't do up his overcoat either. I open the rear door and get in. The interior smells of leather, pipe tobacco, and aftershave.

Dad faces forward wearing blue service dress. A squadron leader's thin band bisecting two thicker ones encircles his cuffs. His pilot's wings and service ribbons are pinned to his chest. He's folded his greatcoat beside him. "Your Aunt Sylvia refused to fly." He releases the brake and navigates through the escalating snow war. Gary sticks out his tongue as Stan Dunlop narrowly misses us with a snowball. Black walnut trees flank the sidewalks, their branches heavy with snow. In the distance a crow caws.

Gary swears and scans the sky. "Bogey, one o'clock high."

I bite my lip.

Thirty feet up, a crow launches from a leafless branch and flies toward us.

Gary presses his face to the glass. "Two o'clock."

Dad turns on the radio. They're playing a serial about some prehistoric monster.

"Three o'clock and closing!"

Dad slows and stops for the sign at Peck Street.

The crow caws again. It's right over us.

"Please, honk your horn, sir." I grip the door handle, ready for the order to bail out.

Dad turns up the volume and the radio play drones on. Now the narrator is talking about bullets, locomotives, and tall buildings.

Gary pivots to look out the back window as we turn onto Queen Street. We must be going to the train station. After a minute, Gary settles in his seat. "All clear, Louise."

The crow lands on a white-sided bungalow and pecks at something in the eavestrough.

Slowly, I relax.

When we get to the station, Dad parks close to the platform. Snow banks ring the shovelled walkways. A flock of starlings flies recon. A uniformed porter with an empty trolley stands sentinel by the tracks. Dad's Sixty Special pings twice. When the train approaches the level crossing, Dad opens his door and steps outside, taking his greatcoat with him. Gary follows.

I scan the skies, and when I'm sure there are no crows in sight, I go, too.

The train chuffs into the station, pulled by one of the new diesel engines. The uniformed porter pushes his trolley to the baggage car. A conductor opens a door, hops down, and sets a wooden step on the platform.

Aunt Sylvia is the first passenger to disembark. She's tucked her red curls into a grey pillbox hat and wears a dark Persian-lamb coat. Her black dress is unwrinkled. Her matching pumps, unscuffed. She smiles, cocks a hip, and opens her arms wide. "How does a girl get a hug around here?"

Gary rushes forward and squeezes her tight.

The conductor assists a mother with a pram. Men in business suits put on their hats and walk around.

Finally, Aunt Sylvia disengages from Gary and smiles at me. "Your turn, Louise."

I step into her embrace. She smells of tropical flowers, cigarette smoke, and wool. She's bonier than Mom and slightly shorter.

"You brought your own typewriter?" Dad eyes the porter's trolley piled high with matching suitcases, a trunk, and a typewriter case.

Aunt Sylvia releases me and looks at Dad. "McGill University was kind enough to switch me to correspondence, Robert." She doesn't blink.

Dad lights his pipe then motions for the porter to follow him to the parking lot. Gary falls in line.

Before I can join them, Aunt Sylvia touches my sleeve, leans close, and whispers. "Louise, you should never pair pink with red."

I clasp my hands behind my back. "No, ma'am."

Aunt Sylvia winks. "Dressing sharp encourages the eager beavers to take notice." She grabs my hand and leads me to where Dad and Gary watch the porter load her luggage. "Are we all set, Robert?" When Dad doesn't answer, Aunt Sylvia opens the driver's door and slides in, the seams on her stockings perfectly straight. She waits for Dad to tip the porter then holds out her hand for the keys.

⌒

0734 hours, 2 March 1951 (Friday)

WE'RE DRIVING DAD ACROSS THE road to the airfield. A US Air Force C-47 Skytrain waits on the tarmac, its twin propellers silent and still. The day is overcast and thirty-five with a slight breeze from the southwest. Aunt Sylvia promised to drive us to school after we've said good-bye. I'm wearing my grey wool dress and last year's Mary Janes. They pinch a little. Gary is dressed in a plaid shirt and rolled up jeans along with my winter boots.

As we approach the access road, the five scarecrows flap in the breeze. Aunt Sylvia glances at Dad. "They're like gibbets, Robert." She wears a camel coat over a white blouse and grey pencil skirt with seamed stockings.

Dad powers down his window and gazes over the barren cornfields next to our house. The incoming breeze carries the scent of wet pavement, humid air, and sour grass. Dad's tires thrum beneath us. The inside temperature drops quickly. He's wearing his greatcoat.

"Who do I call to take them down?"

Dad turns on the radio — twangy guitars and a waltz beat accompany a lady singing about mockingbirds.

Aunt Sylvia switches the radio off. "Their effectiveness is questionable." She taps her window. At ten o'clock, a crow perches on the middle scarecrow, its eyes closed into the morning sun.

I reach for the door handle, just in case.

Gary bounces in his seat. "Honk your horn."

Aunt Sylvia does. Once, twice.

The crow stays put.

"Why isn't it working?" Gary turns to Dad.

Dad powers up his window but says nothing.

Aunt Sylvia frowns then accelerates beyond the speed limit. The crow slides to nine o'clock, then eight o'clock, seven, and finally six. She turns onto the access road.

Gary leans forward. "Are there any crows in Korea?"

A loose stone plinks our underbelly.

Aunt Sylvia waits for Dad to answer. When he doesn't, she turns to Gary. "Not a single one, kiddo."

Gary rests his head on the front seat as we pass the hangars. "Are you sure?"

Aunt Sylvia locks eyes with Gary in the rear-view mirror. "We looked it up in the encyclopaedia last night after you went to bed. Didn't we, Louise?"

My hair follicles bristle. We'd done no such thing. We'd gone through my closet to select today's outfit, but that was it. However, when Gary smiles and settles back in his seat, I realize the only thing I can do is nod.

Aunt Sylvia parks beside the terminal building. Enlisted men salute. Gary and I unload Dad's kit bag, then wait behind the chain link fence as he boards the Skytrain and the engines start. We all wave and try to smile when it takes off.

⁓

1512 hours, 2 March 1951 (Friday)

Gary, me, and fifteen farm kids sit on School Bus 12, waiting for Mr. Gaglioni to finish with Miss Hoekstra. She's pinching Stan Dunlop's left ear. All the other buses have left, but Mr. Gaglioni braked when Stan threw a slushball at our windshield. Mr. Gaglioni's face is red. So is Stan's. The inside of the bus smells like wet wool, stale sweat, and the bruised apple someone left behind this morning.

I wipe my palm across the fogging glass.

Gary reaches over my shoulder. "Open the window so we can hear."

I push his hands away. "Mr. Gaglioni said not to."

Finally, Miss Hoekstra drags Stan toward the school and Mr. Gaglioni reboards the bus. "That's what happens when you do stupid things." He claps his hands and takes his seat. No one makes a sound. Mr. Gaglioni restarts the bus.

Outside, Dad's Sixty Special rushes to the curb. Aunt Sylvia jumps out. Her pencil skirt rides above her knees.

Frank Wilson, a boy in my grade who smells like cheese, lets loose with a wolf whistle.

Mr. Gaglioni spins around. "You want to walk home, Frankie?"

Frank shuts up and slinks down in his seat. He lives two concession roads farther out than we do.

Aunt Sylvia waves to Miss Hoekstra.

Miss Hoekstra drags Stan by his ear to where Aunt Sylvia waits on the sidewalk. They speak briefly, then Miss Hoekstra points at our bus.

Aunt Sylvia waves to Mr. Gaglioni.

Mr. Gaglioni opens the door. "You want something, miss?"

Aunt Sylvia clutches her purse in her gloved hands. "Excuse me, driver, do you have Gary and Louise Martin on your bus? I'm their aunt, Sylvia Forbes."

Mr. Gaglioni nods and calls us forward. Everyone goes *woo* under their breath. Frank Wilson snickers. "What a dish."

Gary balls a fist. "Shut up, Frank."

Everyone's *woo*s get louder.

I push Gary down the aisle before he can do anything stupid.

Mr. Gaglioni claps his hands again and the bus falls silent.

Gary and I form up before Aunt Sylvia. She smiles at Mr. Gaglioni and motions for him to leave. He closes the door, grinds the bus into gear, and drives away. Frank Wilson blows us a kiss. Miss Hoekstra drags Stan into the school. Aunt Sylvia's smile fades. "No one told me there's a bus."

Gary and I look at each other.

"I drove all this way." Aunt Sylvia leads us to Dad's Sixty Special. Gary takes the back seat.

I get in the front and fold my hands in my lap.

Aunt Sylvia takes a deep breath then pats my hand. "We might as well salvage the trip. Is there a good place to eat around here?"

Gary and I look at each other again. We never eat out.

"Nothing too fancy, but still table service."

I relax my hands. "Sterling's has a tea room."

Aunt Sylvia winks at me and starts the engine.

Gary leans forward. "You're not angry?"

Aunt Sylvia glances at him in the rear-view mirror. "Nope." She mugs for Gary until he smiles. "I'm hoping for a good omelette and a fruit cup. What would you two like?"

"A hot dog!" Gary bounces in the back seat.

I smile for Aunt Sylvia. "An omelette sounds nice, ma'am."

∽

1530 hours, 5 March 1951 (Monday)

THE SNOW HAS MELTED BY the time the school bus brings us home. Gary glares at Frank Wilson as Mr. Gaglioni drives away. In the bus's wake, the air smells like dissipating exhaust, thawing mud, and rejuvenating grass. Both Gary and I are wearing the new boots Aunt Sylvia bought us at Sterling's.

Aunt Sylvia waits for us on the porch, her pastel suit, crisp. She's parked Dad's Sixty Special under the catalpa tree. When

I climb the porch, she offers me three small paper-wrapped packages, shaped like books. "For the eager beavers." She's also holding a white cowboy hat, complete with tassels.

I accept her gift. "Thank you, ma'am." The packages are too light to be books.

Gary springs up the steps. "Dad always parks in the carport."

"With your dad's tools lying about, I'd get a run in my stockings for sure." Aunt Sylvia gives Gary the hat. "Unpack the car for me, kiddo?"

Gary thanks her for the hat, jams it on his head, and skips down the steps.

I turn to follow.

"Louise?" Aunt Sylvia indicates the packages. "Aren't you going to open them?"

"Yes, ma'am." I unwrap the paper to find nylon stockings, a white garter belt, and a pair of hosiery gloves.

Aunt Sylvia holds the door open. "Come inside. There's a trick to putting them on."

Gary pushes past me with two grocery sacks in his arms and shakes his head. "Why did you buy milk and eggs?" A third grocery sack remains on the front seat.

Aunt Sylvia frowns. "You don't drink milk?"

Gary sets the sacks on the foyer table. "The milkman comes tomorrow."

Aunt Sylvia rolls her eyes. "Of course he does."

Gary goes back to Dad's Sixty Special while I take the groceries to the kitchen to unpack. Milk, eggs, cheese slices. A bag of onions. Some potatoes. Beans. Tinned peaches. Tea.

Gary enters with the last sack. Store-bought bread. Cans of tomato soup. Sugar. Flour. Butter. And two chocolate bars.

Aunt Sylvia nods. "Go ahead, it won't spoil your dinner."

Gary tears open the wrapping and stuffs chocolate in his mouth. "You didn't get bacon. Or tuna."

Aunt Sylvia puts the soup in the cupboard. "I don't eat meat."

"What?" Gary stops chewing.

I try to shush my brother, but Aunt Sylvia bends to look him in the eye. "I'm vegetarian, kiddo."

Gary's shoulders slump. "Oh."

Aunt Sylvia touches my shoulder. "Shall we try those stockings, Louise? Bring the gloves."

"Yes, ma'am." As we close the cupboards, I hear the far-off burst of a crow.

"I got it." Gary races down the hall holding his new hat to his head, his unbuttoned overcoat winging out behind him. His footfalls clump up the stairs to his bedroom then come down straight away. He opens the front door with a bang and works the lever of his BB gun.

Aunt Sylvia turns off the light switch. "What's that noise?"

I slip my hands behind my back. "He's loading his gun, ma'am."

"His what?" Aunt Sylvia rushes to the front door.

I leave the stockings and gloves on the table and follow.

Two crows sit in the lower branches of the catalpa, directly over Dad's Sixty Special.

My hair follicles stand on end.

Gary fires. His shot grazes the trunk a foot below the crows. Bark flakes off and rains on the windshield.

The crows flex their wings.

Aunt Sylvia gasps. "Did your father buy you that?"

I estimate the distance for Gary. "Nine yards." Well within range. I wet a finger and test the wind. "Slight breeze from the west."

Aunt Sylvia stares at me, open-mouthed.

"Thanks." Gary sights carefully and fires again. A direct hit on a black leg.

The stricken crow squawks and drops from its branch. Halfway to the ground, it beats its wings to slow its descent, then lands on Dad's Sixty Special, right over the passenger window. It tells Gary off in a harsh voice.

Aunt Sylvia's face pales. "Oh my God."

Gary reloads.

"Don't you dare." Aunt Sylvia steps forward.

Gary fires. He hits the crow square in the chest.

With a guttural cry, the crow leaps into the air and flies right at us, pumping its wings hard. Its eyes are black marbles.

"Get inside." Aunt Sylvia opens the door and pushes me in.

Gary works the lever and loads another BB.

"Leave the crows alone!" Aunt Sylvia grabs Gary's arm and drags him into the house.

"Let me shoot them!" Gary tries to twist loose.

The crow pulls up at the last second, disappearing over the porch. Its wing beats sound like an artillery barrage. The second crow rattles ominously.

Aunt Sylvia wraps both arms around Gary. Her eyes are wide. "A little help, Louise?"

"Ma'am?" I bite my lip.

Aunt Sylvia's suit stretches taut, rising to her thighs. "Stop calling me *ma'am*. I'm not in the army."

I clasp my hands behind my back. "What can I do?"

"Take the damned gun away from him before the crows snap their caps."

Gary drags Aunt Sylvia toward the door. "I can get them."

The clips pops loose from Aunt Sylvia's left stocking and it slumps down her leg.

Outside, the first crow returns to the catalpa. Together, the pair glare at our house and send out a rapid series of caws.

Gary's hat falls to the floor. "Let me go!"

"Louise, now!" Aunt Sylvia pins his arms.

I step forward and pry Gary's fingers open.

Aunt Sylvia takes his gun.

Gary spins away and picks up his hat. Tears stream down his cheeks as he faces me. "Traitor!" He thumps up the stairs and slams his door. The whole house rocks.

Aunt Sylvia fixes her stocking then locks the front door and pulls me close. Her heart is beating almost as fast as mine.

∽

0856 hours, 11 March 1951 (Sunday)

AUNT SYLVIA SETS THE TABLE while I spoon pancake batter into the frying pan before church. We're wearing Mom's aprons to protect our brand-new belted navy dresses. Aunt Sylvia says I'll get used to the stockings before long and then they'll stop being so itchy and hot. A warm breeze jets through the window screens, bringing the scents of growing grass, drying wood, and freshly ploughed earth. The two crows bicker in the catalpa. Aunt Sylvia keeps switching records on the hi-fi to drown them out. Nat King Cole, Muddy Waters, Fats Domino.

Gary slips into the kitchen wearing his red sweater, a tartan bowtie, and his cowboy hat. "I'm going to wash the car."

Aunt Sylvia takes the maple syrup from the refrigerator and places it on the table.

"It's streaked with turds." Gary marches to the front door and puts on his new tennis shoes. "We can't drive to church like that."

I flip a pancake with the spatula. "Breakfast is almost ready."

"I'm not hungry." Gary lets the door slam behind him.

Aunt Sylvia frowns.

After breakfast, I bring the dishes to the sink. Gary still hasn't returned.

Aunt Sylvia runs the hot water. "Go get your brother."

I step into my boots at the front door. They feel cold and slippery through the nylon. Dad's Sixty Special is still a mess. Across the road, Mr. Thane is doing touch-and-goes in his Cessna 120 — coming in for a landing then taking off again without slowing down. Four scarecrows flutter in the wind. The one closest to our house is missing. I scan the yard until I hear the sound of ripping paper in the carport. The crows flutter their wings. I double-time it.

The missing flight suit lies atop its wooden frame, next to a grocery sack and a coverless magazine. Gary has tied off the sleeves and pant cuffs with twine.

I clasp my hands behind my back. "It's time for church."

Gary shrugs and tears a page. Women wearing hats and two-piece dresses flash briefly before he crumples and stuffs them into the flight suit.

"Where did you get the magazine?"

Gary pushes his hat back and tears another page. Headlines crinkle. *Fantaisie des nouveaux tailleurs.*

"You little bastard." I run back to the house, tears brimming my eyes.

Aunt Sylvia is putting Amos Milburn on the hi-fi. "All set?"

I brace my feet shoulder-width apart. "Gary didn't wash the car. He's making a better scarecrow."

Aunt Sylvia turns the hi-fi off and marches to the front door, her heels clicking like small-arms fire. "Gary James Martin!"

I peek over her shoulder.

Gary marches across the yard carrying a shovel, his cowboy hat slung low over his eyes. He halts under the catalpa tree.

The crows scold him from above.

Aunt Sylvia steps onto the porch. "You're making them angry."

Gary shrugs and sinks the shovel into the ground.

The crows flap their wings.

Gary flinches, but keeps digging.

Aunt Sylvia doesn't blink. "Stop that."

Gary drops the shovel and marches back to the carport. He comes out in less than a minute with his retrofitted scarecrow. He's stuffed the grocery sack with the crumpled paper from Mom's magazines and has attached it as a head. He pushes the scarecrow's central post into his hole, packs it with dirt, then tops the head off with his tasselled cowboy hat. He steps back and folds his arms across his chest.

Almost immediately, one of the crows drops from the catalpa and lands on his scarecrow's shoulder. It pecks at the tassels on the hat. A slimy white turd dribbles down the flight suit. The scarecrow sags against its frame.

Gary waves his arms like a ground crewman marshalling a distressed aircraft.

The crow takes off and Gary's scarecrow wobbles. The cowboy hat falls to the ground.

The crow circles Gary then dives at the scarecrow, knocking the grocery sack head to the ground as well.

Gary swears. He picks up the shovel and swings it in the air.

The second crow drops from the catalpa to join its partner in the attack. Together, the two birds rip the decapitated head apart.

Aunt Sylvia pales. "Oh my God."

Gary throws the shovel, but misses the crows by at least a yard. It skids across the grass.

Aunt Sylvia's dress flaps in the breeze. "Get in here!"

Gary shakes his head. "I can do this!"

But then three new crows arrive from over the west field and join the first two in the assault on Gary's scarecrow. The flight suit rips and the scarecrow detaches from its frame.

"You're attracting more!" Aunt Sylvia hugs herself.

Gary runs to retrieve the shovel.

I step outside and use my best parade voice. "Retreat!"

Gary picks up the shovel and charges the crows.

I sprint forward to intercept. I grab his sleeve and drag him back to the house. "You can't scare away the whole flock."

Gary throws the shovel across the porch, where it clatters off the edge and tumbles onto the grass, leaving a gouge mark in the wood. "A flock of crows is called a murder, Louise. Look it up."

I horripilate and push him inside.

Behind us, the crows dance the scarecrow across the yard then pull it into the catalpa. In a frenzy, they tear it apart. Bits of empty flight suit and crumpled paper scatter in the wind.

Aunt Sylvia swats Gary hard across the back of his pants. "Go to your room!"

Red spots fill Gary's cheeks as he reaches for his bottom. "You hit me."

I set my feet shoulder-width apart and cross my arms. "Serves you right."

⁓

1624 hours, 13 March 1951 (Tuesday)

I'M IN THE KITCHEN DICING a carrot when I hear Dad's Sixty Special in the driveway. Aunt Sylvia made Gary go shopping with her at Sterling's as soon as Mr. Gaglioni dropped us off. He's not allowed out of her sight. I got to stay home so I started on dinner. I've peeled and washed three potatoes, opened a tin of peaches, and am now working on a salad. I'm a little unsure what to do next with meat off the menu. I've got an apron over my new pleated skirt.

Two car doors slam and Gary runs across the gravel, bangs open the front door, and pounds up the stairs.

Aunt Sylvia opens the front door. "I had to do it!" Her voice trembles. She enters the kitchen wearing her camel coat over her plaid button-front dress. She sets a grocery sack on the counter. "Louise, please ask your brother to come down." She sits on a chair to take off her shoes and rub her feet.

"Yes, Aunt Sylvia." I wipe my hands on my apron and climb the stairs. Gary's room overlooks the front of the house and his walls are covered with Dad's framed squadron patches. A photo of Mom with her Cessna sits on his desk, along with two of her trophies. They used to be in Dad's study, but Gary stole them after she died and Dad never made him put them back. On his bed is a brand new model kit for an F-86 Sabre.

Gary slides out from under his bed and pulls down his covers. He's wearing his red sweater with rolled-up jeans. "Get out!" He pushes me into the hall. His eyes are wet.

I catch the door with my left hand. "What did you do?"

Gary wipes his eyes with his sleeve. "She threw away my gun."

Through his window, I can see more than ten crows roosting in the still-barren branches of the catalpa tree. Little bits of paper and flight suit litter the lawn. Aunt Sylvia made Dad's cadets take the other flight suits down yesterday. I step back and fold my arms across my chest. "Aunt Sylvia wants you."

Gary puts his hands on his hips. "When Aunt Sylvia thought I was in the washroom, a man at Sterling's told me how to get rid of the crows." Hanging behind him are models of Dad's fighters from World War II — a Hawker Hurricane and a Supermarine Spitfire. They twist slowly on their threads.

Downstairs, Aunt Sylvia slams a pot on the stove. She's making the dinner I wanted to give her.

I drop my arms. "How?"

Gary pulls a shiny whistle from his pocket, the price tag still on it. He opens his window and the mingled scents of wet feathers, sodden dirt, and growing grass fill his room. The crows sound like unsquelched radio static.

"Louise?" Aunt Sylvia calls from the base of the stairs.

I step into Gary's room and close the door.

Gary leans out the window and puts the whistle to his lips.

"Not now, knucklehead." I rush forward and grab the whistle just as Gary blows. The pea throbs in my hand, but thankfully I've muted the sound in time.

Gary wrestles his whistle away from me. "Traitor." He puts the whistle back to his lips.

"Aunt Sylvia will take it away, too." I back up and raise my hands, palms up. "Wait until she's out of the house."

Gary lowers the whistle. "You'll help me?"

I nod. "I hate crows as much as you do."

Aunt Sylvia pushes open Gary's door. She steps inside, silent in her stocking feet. "Where did you get that?" She points at the whistle and doesn't blink.

When Gary doesn't come up with an answer, I step forward. "I won it at school. First prize in an orienteering competition."

Aunt Sylvia frowns then slowly shakes her head. "Don't lie to me, Louise."

I bite my lip.

"Both of you, get your jackets. We're returning it right now."

A Flock of Crows is Called a Murder

Gary leans out his window and blows the whistle as hard as he can. The pea throbs under the blast and my ears hurt as they try to squeeze shut. Outside, the crows fall silent.

"No!" Aunt Sylvia rushes across the room.

Gary's face turns red, but he keeps blowing.

I cover my ears with my hands and move to block Aunt Sylvia.

"Louise, are you insane?" Aunt Sylvia pushes past me.

But it doesn't matter. Even before Aunt Sylvia plucks the whistle from Gary's lips, the crows start up again, louder than before.

⸺

1638 hours, 15 March 1951 (Thursday)

AUNT SYLVIA IS FRANTICALLY TYPING an assignment in the kitchen. She says it has to be in the mail today, so Gary and I are exiled to the living room. Dinner is on hold. The house smells of stagnant air, lemon furniture polish, and Aunt Sylvia's perfume. I'm in my grey wool dress. My nylons are scratchy. I'm standing sentry at the front window, scanning the catalpa with the binoculars. The crows' ranks have swollen to over twenty. Dad's turd-streaked Sixty Special is parked on the grass next to the porch for quick deployment.

Gary, in a sweater vest and corduroy pants, pinches my shoulder. "They do too have crows in Korea." He's got volume six of the encyclopaedia in his hands, *Coleb to Damasci*.

I clasp my hands behind my back. "I know."

"You lied to me."

"It made you feel better."

Gary snaps the book closed and drops it on the chesterfield. "Dad's in danger. Does that make you feel better?"

"No kidding, you little booger. He's at war."

"I mean from the crows."

I bite my lip. "I'm sure the US Air Force has figured out how to keep crows from swarming their jets."

Gary shakes his head. "It doesn't have to be like Mom. At his speeds, all it takes is for one bird to fly into his canopy or get sucked into his air intake."

I close my eyes. "I know."

Aunt Sylvia stops typing and pulls her paper through her typewriter. A moment later, her heels click across the kitchen floor and she pushes open the door. "I should still be able to make it."

I rush into the hall to get her camel coat from the closet.

"Thanks, Louise." Aunt Sylvia licks her envelope closed.

I nod. "Can I start dinner while you're at the post office?"

Aunt Sylvia slips into her coat. "That would be swell." She pushes open the front door and dashes to Dad's Sixty Special.

In the catalpa, the crows flutter and squawk.

Dad's tires spit mud across the grass as Aunt Sylvia speeds away.

Gary marches into the hall and folds his arms across his chest. "Don't ever lie to me again."

I close the door. "I won't. I promise."

Gary runs upstairs. "Be right back."

"What are you getting?" I follow him to his room.

Gary retrieves the Sabre model kit box from under his bed. He opens it and takes out a red-and-white-striped cardboard tube, about two feet long and an inch in diameter. "It's a

Roman candle. The man said to use fireworks if the whistle didn't work."

I check my wristwatch. "Aunt Sylvia will be back in twenty minutes, tops."

Gary frowns.

I step back into the hall. "I'll get the matches." I turn and run down the stairs.

Gary whoops, grabs the Roman candle, and thumps down after me.

I pause outside Dad's study. No one has been in here since he left. I push the door open. The curtains are drawn. Dust swirls in the air. On the walls are framed certificates and photographs. Dad's commission. Dad with the other aces from his squadron in Europe. Dad being decorated by George VI. On his desk are two pictures of Mom. Her first transcontinental race. Their wedding day.

I select a box of matches from the middle drawer.

Back in the hall, Gary waits for me in my winter boots. He's got Mom's flight boots ready for me.

I check my watch again. "Eighteen minutes."

Together we push open the front door and the crows' chatter swells. One or two outriders circle high, but most are roosting in the catalpa.

Gary humps forward and kicks away his old scarecrow's frame. He jams his Roman candle into the hole at a seventy-five-degree angle.

I dash forward, strike a match, and touch it to the wick. The Roman candle hisses and smokes, then the smoke disappears into the cardboard tube and the hissing stops. "It's a dud."

Above us, branches are filled with flapping black wings.

Gary steps closer to look into the Roman candle when the first fireball shoots out, narrowly missing his face. A muted *whuum* sounds and a glowing red ball streaks halfway up the tree, screeching like a top. It winks out in a shower of sparks.

The crows rustle in the tree, but none fly away. The outriders skitter and duck into the uppermost branches.

The next ball *whuum*s up. Smoke hangs blue. The air smells like gunpowder.

The crows fall silent for a moment, then pick up their chatter.

"He promised."

The Roman candle *whuum*s again.

The crows caw and squawk.

Whuum.

Gary starts to cry. "I must have grabbed the wrong kind."

Whuum. As the last ball floats into the sky, a crow dives from the catalpa. Wings whoosh past as it grabs the spent Roman candle and takes it into the tree.

I scream and cover my head, then sprint to the front porch, jumping over the shovel still lying in the grass. The clips on my right leg release and I feel the stocking loosen.

Back at the catalpa, Gary cries out. "Louise!"

I make it to the front door and spin around.

My little brother is crawling across the lawn, his pant leg caught on a nail in the scarecrow frame. Crows drop from the catalpa, swarm, and dive at him, their cawing the wailing sirens of Stuka bombers. Turds fall like unexploded ordnance. Gary pulls his sweater-vest over his head. "Help me!" Mom was on her final approach to the airfield when the murder swarmed her. Crows stuck to her propeller, jammed her control surfaces, and punched through her cockpit. She died in a fiery crash.

I pick up the shovel and run to my little brother, pushing him under my skirt for protection.

He grabs my knees with both hands and kicks free of the wooden frame. His pants rip.

I brandish the shovel like a battleaxe, arcing it over my head. I swing at a crow. "Get lost!" I miss. I swing again. Again. And again. Finally, on my fifth try, I hit one. The shovel crunches and a crow falls. It flutters and shrieks on the ground. I bash its head. Blood splatters over my dress and up my legs. I hit it again.

Gary crawls out from under me and grins. Crow's blood dapples his forehead. "Confirmed kill."

The swarm scatters and retreats to the heights of the catalpa. They settle and rise like touch-and-goes.

I swing the shovel. "Want some more?"

The crows mass again, dip their wings, and dive.

I look down to check Gary. He gives me the thumbs-up. My right stocking is around my ankle and my left is laddered in at least three places. Both are speckled with blood. I pick up the dead crow and hold it above my head. "I'll kill you all!"

The crows stutter and back away.

Gary gets to his feet and takes the shovel. He swings it back and forth while I brandish the corpse.

The crows gain altitude, then bank in unison and retreat over the west field.

When they're out of sight, Gary hugs me. "All clear."

I hug him back.

1243 hours, 25 March 1951 (Easter Sunday)

After church, we pull into our driveway and park beside Mr. Thane's red pickup under the empty branches of the catalpa. A lone contrail swells and dissipates in the cloudless sky. Everything smells like warm car, cool grass, and chocolate-stained brother. Last Friday, Gary and I washed the car and raked the front yard. The past ten days have been a blissful crow-free respite.

Aunt Sylvia and I both wear two-piece dresses, although she's a little put out I won't wear stockings anymore. She and I got up at dawn to hide eggs in the living room. Gary wears a bowtie and a collared shirt. He shared every piece of chocolate he found.

Mr. Thane stands by our porch in a black suit. He takes off his hat and slips a telegram from his pocket. "They sent this to the airfield."

Aunt Sylvia pales.

Mr. Thane forces a thin-lipped smile and lowers his head. "I'm sorry."

Aunt Sylvia stumbles onto the porch and opens the front door. She leads Mr. Thane to the living room and takes a seat on the chesterfield. "Read it, please."

Mr. Thane swallows. "Deeply regret to inform you Squadron Leader Robert G. Martin was killed in action 24 March 1951 in the Korean area in the performance of his duty. Please accept my most heartfelt sympathy in your bereavement. Sorry, no details available at present. Pilots who lose their lives are returned home for burial as soon as possible. Any additional information received will be promptly forwarded."

My hair follicles stand on end.

"No!" Gary sobs and thumps up the stairs. He slams his bedroom door.

Mr. Thane folds the telegram and places it on the coffee table. "I'll let myself out."

Aunt Sylvia sits rigid. Tears brim her eyes. She doesn't blink.

Mr. Thane closes our front door and steps off the porch. He pauses by the catalpa, looks closely, then grimaces and crosses himself.

A second wave of horripilation washes over me.

Mr. Thane steps up to the catalpa and with two quick tugs, takes down the dead crow Gary and I had nailed through the wings to the far side of the trunk. He tosses the desiccated corpse into the back of his pickup, wipes his hands on a rag, then drives away.

⌒

0041 hours, 26 March 1951 (Monday)

HOT TEARS STREAK MY CHEEKS. My face is sore from crying so much. A chill draft whistles into my room from under my door. It smells like cold dirt, wet grass, and bird shit. The crows came back at sunset. Mr. Thane is an idiot. I slip out of bed and step into the hall. "Gary?" He'd knocked on my door a little while ago, but I hadn't been ready to deal with anyone yet, so I'd pretended I hadn't heard.

His door is closed. The draft is coming from his room.

I tap with my fingertips. "You still awake?"

He doesn't answer.

I push open his door and bite my lip. Gary's window is wide open and his curtains billow into his room. The Hurricane and the Spitfire spin in ragged circles on their threads. Pieces of the new F-86 lie smashed on his desk. His covers are bunched into a ball. I touch his mattress. It's cold. Mom's picture lies on his wrinkled sheets.

I look under his bed. It's empty.

I slow march to the window. The catalpa is silhouetted black against the silvery moon, looking like a prehistoric monster breathing in the night as it seethes with roosting crows. There must be over one hundred of them.

My eyes sweep the front yard, hoping to spot my brother advancing on the catalpa with the shovel, ready to engage them. I don't see him, but what I do find makes me horripilate again. The dew has already fallen and Gary's footprints are clearly defined in the moonlit grass. They trace a direct course to the airfield. I grab the binoculars from my room and search for a full minute. I'm just about to give up when I hear the cough of an engine starting. And then a whine. A buzz. It's a Cessna 120. I race downstairs.

Aunt Sylvia is still on the chesterfield. The lights are off.

I grab her hand. "Gary's at the airfield."

Aunt Sylvia doesn't blink, doesn't look at me, doesn't react at all. Her cheeks are streaked with mascara.

I run to the closet, grab Mom's boots, and jam them on my feet. I throw open the front door, letting it crash against the wall. The crows caw and squawk, fluttering their wings in agitation. I jump off the porch and swear at them as I run across the lawn.

At the airfield, a plane lurches toward the runway. No red and green flashes blink from the wingtips — it's Mr. Thane's Cessna.

A Flock of Crows is Called a Murder

"Gary! Don't!" I try to jump across the ditch but slip on the far side and slide back into the cold water. I climb out and sprint to the chain-link fence surrounding the terminal building, but it's no use. Mr. Thane's Cessna 120 wobbles down the runway, picks up speed, and takes off. I'm too late.

The High Alpinist's Survival Guide

You must respect the rules of the high alpine if you want to survive Everest.
— Scott Turner, *The High Alpinist's Survival Guide*

9:36 PM, April 30
Camp IV, South Col

I'm making a double batch of tomato soup in my tent, with freeze-dried ham and tortellini. On my stove. No one calls it a titanium burner, Dad. The one time I did, five years ago, Christine laughed at me. That was my sixteenth-birthday Mount Logan ascent. The two of you gave me a signed copy of *The High Alpinist's Survival Guide* at the summit. I haven't cooked in a sealed tent since.

Phurba Gelu Sherpa says *golep pep* and slips his oxygen mask over his face. He's leaving me.

I remind him we've been together for a month — Kathmandu, Lukla, the trek to Namche Bazaar, then on to Base Camp, across the Khumbu Icefall, through the Western Cwm, and up Lhotse Face.

Phurba slides on his outer hood.

I point out he's known you for twenty years. Together, you've attempted every 8,000 metre peak in the Himalaya.

He indicates the collapsible sled jutting from my pack. "You lie, Brian Turner."

I lift the pot lid. Chunks of snow iceberg the surface. You always preached against powdered food, arguing if it doesn't taste good at home, it'll taste like shit on the mountain. I'd told Phurba I was summiting Everest because you never did. Now, I tell him the truth.

Phurba pulls his double mitts over his gloves. "Your life not matter to you?"

My life matters to me very much. "I'll double your contract. Ninety thousand. American." Mom can afford it.

Phurba unzips my doorflap and crawls outside. Wind swells my tent and flickers my stove. *"Golep pep."* He reseals my door, leaving three inches for a cooking vent.

You're on the Hillary Step. The Balcony, the South Summit, and the Cornice Traverse still separate us. Up here, the air is so thin it's incapable of sustaining human life, so without Phurba, my odds shrink exponentially. "One hundred thousand!"

Outside, I hear another zipper, then a shallow cough, metal clink on rock, and more zippers. The commercial expeditions are leaving early, but poaching one of their Sherpas would be tantamount to murder — their clients are paying tourists, not experienced alpinists. Careful not to upset my stove, I unzip my door flap. Three metres away, fifteen other tents barnacle the exposed plateau. Bobbing headlamps occlude Phurba's silhouette as he approaches the tent he shares with Tendi, another Sherpa. "One hundred fifty!"

Phurba ignores me and crawls inside.

Between us, a woman squats to the left of her entrance vestibule, a roll of toilet paper in her hand. "Like what you see?" She has a slight American accent.

I'm not looking at her exposed ass — it's the rusted tent pole beneath her mess that's caught my attention. *Was it from your last summit bid?*

Toilet Paper Woman's crampons screech on the loose shale as she covers herself and turns off her headlamp. I doubt she even recognizes the dangers of contaminating camp snow.

I consider my satphone but decide against it. Even if I could find a replacement Sherpa, the summer monsoons will close the climbing window before he could get here. I grab a handful of clean snow from the sack by my door and duck inside. I can't afford to give up.

෴

The majority of climbers are left where they fall.
— Scott Turner, *The High Alpinist's Survival Guide*

෴

10:27 PM, April 30
200 metres above Camp IV

The first commercial expedition is above me, bunched at the top of a fixed rope, their dotted headlamps effervescing fireflies. Wind ripples my black outer shell. Blown snow dazzles my headlamp.

The tourists trust their equipment far too much, letting the ropes support their full weight. Climber inexperience. Once the first expedition detaches, I feed the rope through my jumar and ascend quickly. The second expedition clips on and leans back, twanging the rope from my hands. I grab the rope again and scramble up before they can pull out the ice screws. At the top, I detach and start trudging, my boots crunching snow.

Twenty metres later I stop for a handful of breaths and look down. The second expedition is strung out in pairs along the fixed rope. Below them, the moon rises over the clouds. I pat my pack and feel my spare rope and ice axe. Inside are my requisite four oxygen bottles and the collapsible sled. My knife is in an outer pocket. The satphone, two thermoses, a chocolate bar, and my extra water are in my down suit.

I take a step. A breath. Another step.

Thirty metres up, a headlamp from the first expedition drops and an instinctive scream echoes down the slope. The tourist is falling directly along my ascent path.

I swear and free my ice axe. I push the spiked end into the snow, then hunch to my knees. If I get injured, this is all over.

The headlamps of the other tourists turn, but none of them go down — no one must be tied to the falling climber. Leader negligence. The scream dopplers higher.

I tuck my shoulder against the shaft of my axe and brace myself for the coming impact.

The falling tourist skids closer, accelerating. "Help me!" A woman's voice, slight American accent. Could be Toilet Paper Woman.

My headlamp reflects spraying powder. "Tuck your arms in!" I shout. "Dig with your knees!"

She kicks at the mountain, obviously untrained in self-arrest.

"Lift your feet!" I shout again. "Use your knees!"

She digs her feet down hard.

"Your crampons will snag!"

It happens as I say it. Her left foot catches on a rock and her leg buckles. She somersaults, then hits her head on another rock and her scream aborts. She spins away from me and her body tumbles safely by the hunched-in second expedition, finally coming to a stop below the fixed rope.

The first expedition watches for two minutes and forty-three seconds. When the fallen climber doesn't move in that time, they turn and resume their climb, followed by their Sherpas. Everyone on the mountain understands rescue attempts above 8,000 metres have little chance of success, and with inexperienced rescuers, the likely result will be their deaths as well. The second expedition doesn't stop.

"You okay?" I call down but get no response. I watch for six more minutes, but still the fallen climber doesn't move. When the second expedition begins to detach at the top of the fixed rope, I take three deep breaths and move on.

∽

Without sufficient oxygen, both your body and your brain will begin to shut down.
— Scott Turner, *The High Alpinist's Survival Guide*

∽

5:44 AM, May 1
The Balcony

Dawn. Below me, Everest's shadow ghosts on the clouds roiling over the lesser peaks of the Himalaya. Across from me, the sun flares on the curving horizon. Above me, Everest's South Summit blushes in the thin light.

I take a deep breath but get nothing. I squeeze my oxygen mask, unclogging the ice buildup, and try again. I get something this time, but not enough. The air feels empty. I check my regulator — two litres per minute. At that flow rate, I should have six hours of oxygen. Seven-hundred twenty litres per bottle, three more bottles in my pack. The numbers are confusing, won't stay still. I try to suck in more air — two, three, four breaths, but none are thick enough. I can't fill my lungs. Claustrophobia onrushes. My heart beats too fast. I try to concentrate on other things — the cold, my itchy scalp, the salty taste of sweat on my lip. I take another step. Another. Three more steps. Twelve more empty breaths. No idea how many heartbeats. When a flat ledge opens before me, I stop. A wind gust buffets my hood. Twirling snow dances over the rocks.

Under the ledge, the wind has gouged a shallow cave. My headlamp flashes on purple. It must be another fallen climber. Five steps and I'm there. My chest throbs. My head swirls. Sweat stings my eyes. I take three shallow breaths, lean on my ice axe, and kneel. "You okay?" Most people understand that word, no matter which language they speak.

No response.

My vision darkens. Like a tunnel. I gasp. Two more empty breaths. I pull out my watch. 6:05 AM. I left after ten last night. I do the math again. Eight hours of climbing. Six hours of oxygen. This time the numbers stay put. My oxygen bottle is empty.

I spin off my regulator. Three breaths. Oxygen hisses as I attach a new bottle. I up the flow rate to four litres per minute.

The air thickens. My head clears. The closeness subsides. My heart relaxes.

Reflected sunlight brightens the cave. I turn off my headlamp and stow it in my pack. The purple is from an older-style outer shell — Christine Wood. You let me meet her after you summitted Annapurna together when I was twelve, then made me promise never to tell. Christine would tie my knots whenever my hands got too cold. I never meant to hurt her.

The first expedition, whom I'd passed an hour ago, arrives. They're in matching blue outer shells with American flags loud on their sleeves. None of them acknowledge either me or Christine as they trek past. I give myself five minutes of double oxygen before dialling back. I take out my first thermos and drink warm soup.

Christine died three years ago in a sudden overnight storm. The next morning, you gave up on the summit and came down alone, telling people you couldn't wake her. Her gloves and mitts are gone, exposing her skin grafts. Her scarf is missing, too — the one you bought for her in Lukla twenty years ago after her first 8,000 metre peak — the one she never took off.

I finish my soup, stow my thermos, and stand. Just the South Summit and the Cornice Traverse to go.

⌇

Climbers can burn over six-thousand calories per day. Have convenient calorie-dense foods with you at all times.
 — Scott Turner, *The High Alpinist's Survival Guide*

⌇

7:22 AM, May 1
South Summit

Two blue tourists bargain-bin a cache of oxygen bottles. One is tall and sinewy, the other short and muscular — a basketball centre and a football linebacker. Tendi, their Sherpa, squats to the side, his focus elsewhere.

Basketball Centre leans on his axe. Wheezes. "Can't go on."

Above, the true summit burns against the dark sky. One hundred metres to go. The rest of the first expedition has gone on ahead.

Linebacker disconnects his oxygen bottle and drops it in the cache.

"Don't mix the spent bottles with the full," I say. Common sense.

Linebacker shrugs and selects another bottle.

I keep climbing. One step. Two breaths. One step. Two breaths.

Linebacker drops a second bottle. "Empty." He grabs another.

I shake my head. All of my oxygen is with me. I don't cache.

Basketball Centre drops to a knee. "So tired."

I trudge over and give him my chocolate bar.

He tears it open and takes a bite. Wind snatches the wrapper and rockets it into the clouds. "Your father," he pauses for a breath, looks up at me, "belongs," he breathes again, "on," breath, "Everest."

Phurba's got a big mouth. "You read my dad's book?"

Basketball Centre nods and pats his pack. "Got it with me."

I turn to Tendi. "Get them down."

Linebacker picks up another bottle.

I leave them and follow the knife-edge ridge of the Cornice Traverse up from the South Summit, forty metres behind the rest of their expedition. They're single file on a fixed rope, no room to pass. A misstep to the right is a 3,000 metre fall into China. A misstep to the left, 2,400 metres deeper into Nepal. Mount Everest is not a beautiful place. It's a treacherous fucking netherworld, littered with the dead. I wait for the blue tourists to get off the rope. My shins ache. So does my spine. All I hear is my breath filling my heat-exchanging mask. All I smell is stale sweat, tomato, and reconstituted ham. My eyelashes are freezing. My glacier glasses fog up. I clear them with my mitts.

When the first expedition finally detaches, I clip on and tug. The closest ice screw holds. I feed the rope through my jumar and cross the ridge quickly.

∽

The Hillary Step is the last technical challenge before the summit.
— Scott Turner, *The High Alpinist's Survival Guide*

∽

8:36 AM, May 1
The Hillary Step
The twelve-metre snow-blasted wall is webbed with ropes, both recent and fraying. A mash of footprints marks the base. As I approach, the last ascending blue tourist swings over the top. I find you at the bottom, your head twisted to the left, still clipped to an old rope. Your prototype crampons are bent, the titanium too light to be durable. The company you tested them for folded when news of your fall spread.

Your sun-faded orange outer shell has been ripped apart. The same for your insulated suit. Corporate logos and tufts of down flutter in the wind. After Logan, you had to get creative with your fundraising. Beneath your shredded clothing, your chest is the colour of marble. Someone has crossed your arms. Prayer flags and abandoned gear surround you. Your name and the date from two years ago has been scratched into a spent oxygen bottle. Christine's purple scarf is tied around your right arm like a favour. You came back the year after she died to make a last summit attempt, solo. Since then, climbers post pictures on the Internet. Journalists request interviews. At Grandma's funeral last year, I asked Mom if I could get you down in exchange for forgiveness. She said yes.

Your oxygen mask comes off with a crack, snapping near the buckles. Under your orange balaclava, you've got a month's worth of silver beard and a deep gash on your temple. Your skin is white — a quick death. Frostbitten skin turns black.

I take out my knife, cut Christine's scarf free, and stuff it in an outer pocket.

A male voice grunts behind me. "Looting," breath, "the dead?" British accent.

I whirl around, knife in hand, still on my knees.

It's a tourist from the second expedition. Red outer shell. Union Jack on his shoulder. He stands over me like a bulldog.

"My father." I put my knife away.

Bulldog pats his side pocket. "Brilliant book."

An expedition leader is tied to him, wearing gold. "We're on a schedule, mate." Kiwi accent, not Aussie. He pauses for two breaths. "You want time on the summit for photos."

More tourists arrive, an eclectic mix sporting flags from four continents, safety ropes pairing them off. A black and white panda with a pink flamingo, a yellow cheetah and a brown raccoon — a multi-coloured box of animal crackers. Their Sherpas, Lhakpa and Dorji, follow.

"Satphone good?" Panda asks with a thick Cantonese accent. His breath shoots out in clouds.

Kiwi pats his pack. "You can call the wife," breath, "from the top of the world."

While the animal crackers untie their safety ropes, I cut you from the old rope.

"You're really," Flamingo pauses for a breath, "taking him down?"

I don't bother to answer as I unpack my sled, extend it, and slide you on top.

"He dedicated his book to you," Cheetah says. She's svelte and lean.

To C.W. and B.T., trusted partners in the high alpine.

Raccoon leans close, lifts his dark goggles. "Not the third," breath, "edition." He's round with small hands.

Mom never knew before Mount Logan. When she married you, her name was Charlotte Weathers, so you always had plausible deniability. After Logan, you removed the B.T. and made partner singular. I hold up my left hand. I know the Sherpas understand beneath my mitts, I'm shooting the finger at their clients.

Lhakpa and Dorji shrug and help the animal crackers clip on. Kiwi first, then Bulldog, followed by Flamingo, Panda, Cheetah, and Raccoon — the same order as before. By the time I'm done lashing you to the sled, they're up and over the Hillary Step.

༄

You should be accustomed to spending long periods at high altitudes on your own.
— Scott Turner, *The High Alpinist's Survival Guide*

༄

11:43 AM, May 1
Cornice Traverse

The jet stream batters my ears. My outer shell snaps like black bubble wrap. My shoulders burn and my mouth tastes like stale ham. I'm dragging you across the knife-edge ridge, the sled tied to my pack with my spare rope — a jury-rigged harness. To our left is the drop into China. To our right, Nepal. In the distance are the brown plains of the Tibetan Plateau. I pull, breathe, and step, feed the rope through my jumar, and pull again. I can feel my heartbeat in my throat.

When we get to the first anchor point, I stop and detach. I step around the ice screw and bend to reconnect my jumar. A sudden lull in the wind off-balances me. As I pitch forward, our connecting rope slackens and you slip off the ridge, China side. I scramble to brace my feet, but my crampons gnash on rock and I slip.

You hit the end of the rope. Hard.

My harness tightens. Hard.

The buffeting wind returns. Hard.

With no solid footing, I fall. My hip slams into rock and I hear cracking sounds from an inner pocket. I don't think it's ribs, but I don't have time to investigate. I reach for the fixed rope and catch it in my mitts.

You keep sliding, dragging us toward China.

I try to brace my crampons, but only find rock. There's nothing to dig into. I reach for the fixed rope and try to clip on. It tightens, then, with a crack, the ice screw disengages and the rope slips from my hands.

Still sliding backward, you pull me over the edge.

I free my ice axe, not bothering with the wrist leash. Careful to avoid rock, I hack at the mountain. The teeth of the curved pick bite into loose snow and we keep sliding.

I jab again. More snow.

And again. Snow.

Again. This time, my axe punctures ice and holds. I tighten my grip but you keep dragging me down. My mitts slip over the shaft.

Dislodged rocks avalanche down the mountain as we slide. I dig in with my knees, ripping my outer shell but not finding the purchase I need. I punch the snow, looking for a handhold. A few more metres and I find a tiny spur of limestone. I grab as tight as I can and manage to arrest our descent. My fingers burn with the strain. A muted rumble rises from the falling rocks below.

I look up to the Hillary Step, hoping to see descending tourists, someone I can ask for help, but it's bare. Both commercial expeditions must still be on the summit, calling loved ones and corporate sponsors while posing for photos.

I consider removing my pack and letting you fall, but dismiss the thought. Mom wants you away from Everest. I dig my crampons into the snow, alleviating my straining fingers.

The High Alpinist's Survival Guide

I consider my satphone again, but Base Camp is over a day away — too far for a rescue. I'm on my own. I shake my head and smile. You were wrong about the importance of following the rules. The key to success on any mountain is simply unrelenting determination.

I rotate onto my back and dig in with my heels. My crampons hold. I feel the strain though my feet, even down to where my toes used to be — frostbite from that night on Logan. Forty breaths later I start to climb, kicking and punching as I go. I ensure each handhold is perfect. I pull you up. Ten minutes and most of my strength later, I recover my ice axe and together we tumble into the rutted path on top of the ridge. I clip on to the fixed rope and secure the ice screw. My heart is racing. I sit for twenty minutes until it slows. I stare at you and wonder how a simple blood pump ever got associated with love in the first place. It wasn't in your book.

༄

One in twenty Everest climbers will die in their summit attempt.

— Scott Turner, *The High Alpinist's Survival Guide*

༄

1:28 PM, May 1
South Summit

I'm on my second-last oxygen bottle. My shoulders are raw — they've got to be bleeding. Cold air finds its way through the rip in my outer shell, biting my left knee. My muscles quiver intermittently. Thinking is getting harder. Both the blue Americans and the animal crackers catch up at the oxygen cache.

Kiwi trudges by, panting. "Why bust," breath, breath, "your guts?" He trades spent bottles for fresh ones with his tourists.

"I promised."

The blue expedition leader is a woman. Texas accent. Biggest pack on the mountain. She throws a bottle to the rocks. "Some of these," breath, "are empty." She swears at me.

I unstrap my harness. My shoulders scream. "Your clients," breath, "did that."

"His book," she points at you, "says to always separate." She picks up another bottle, tests it, then pitches it over the edge.

"You've got it with you?" I ask.

Blue Texan finds another bad bottle. "My entire team carries it."

I point at the safety ropes joining the animal crackers. "Your team isn't tied in."

Blue Texan shrugs. "If one falls," breath, "two get pulled down."

"Not if you've done your job and taught them to self-arrest."

Blue Texan makes a fist and steps toward me.

Kiwi intercepts her. "Don't waste the energy, mate."

The tourists collect around their leaders. Flamingo leans forward. "Why are you," breath, "moving him?" The Sherpas hang back.

I look at their faces. Some are hostile, most are eager. With a cautious descent, they'll be in Base Camp the day after tomorrow, Kathmandu next week. Home the day after that. "My mother wants him buried."

Kiwi stares. "But this is Everest."

I point at you. "Give me a hand?"

Both leaders shake their heads.

"I can pay," I say. "Fifty thousand." When that doesn't entice them, I add, "Each."

Blue Texan breathes a few times then forbids her team from accepting my offer.

"One hundred thousand."

Raccoon and Bulldog express interest until Kiwi proscribes my money, too.

Mom said if I didn't get you down, I could forget about coming home. Ever. "I've got to do this."

Blue Texan kicks the snow. "Then we'll see you next season." She makes the sign of the cross. "Under a snow drift."

I shoot her the finger.

Blue Texan turns and walks away, followed by her team and the animal crackers. Not even the Sherpas look back.

࿇

Wounds don't heal at altitude, they worsen.
— Scott Turner, *The High Alpinist's Survival Guide*

࿇

6:03 PM, May 1
The Balcony

Sunset. Clouds form to the west and the wind calms. Twilight won't last long but the tourists have left a trail of churned footprints and spent oxygen bottles so I can't get lost. I attach my last oxygen bottle.

I'm losing feeling in my fingers. My cheeks have got to be frostnipped. Same with my exposed knee. My sweat no longer tastes salty. I lower you over the Balcony and you land with a jolt near the cave. I drop over the ledge, lean into my harness, and pull. You don't budge. My shoulders are numb. I pull again, a different angle. You're caught on something. It's too dark to see what.

I put on my headlamp and turn it on. Your sled is snagged on Christine's right boot. I'd tried to make freeze-dried chilli for dinner that night, but I forgot to leave a vent. You freaked, told me the titanium burner was sucking the oxygen from the tent, said I'd never learn the rules. I panicked, knocked over the stove, and set the tent on fire. Christine pulled me out. I tried to help her, but you pushed me away, said I'd done enough. While you treated her burns, Christine asked me to call in a rescue. I powered on the satphone, punched in the speed dial, and Mom answered. You called me a fucking idiot, over and over again. Christine said third-degree burns and Mom finally knowing was better than me being dead. You had nothing to say to that. When the helicopter arrived at sunset, you took Christine and the satphone and told the pilot I'd stay to pack up our gear. Mom made the rescue team come back at dawn. They flew me directly to the hospital in Anchorage. When I got home to West Vancouver a month later, Mom stopped talking to me and sent me to live with Grandma in Ontario. By then, you'd already moved into Christine's Kitsilano apartment. Christine sent me birthday cards every year, but you never signed them. I duck into the cave and tie Christine's scarf over her hands. I really miss her.

I lever your sled off Christine's leg and pull. You slide forward until your shoulder catches on a rock. I pull harder. Your outer shell rips and your skin tears, exposing grey muscle beneath. You stop moving. I pull again and lose my footing, slipping to the ground. My oxygen bottle tinks on another rock. Mom bought a plot next to Grandma's in Ontario — a newly consecrated repurposed cornfield with no mountains in sight — our way of saying fuck you.

I get up and pull again, leaning into my makeshift harness. More of your skin tears away. I kick your sled, jolting you from the rock, and pull. You slide clear. I take a step, stop, breathe seven times, then step again. My air feels light. I look, but there's no blockage to unclog. I up the flow rate to maximum but nothing gets through. I check the bottle — it's hissing. The valve is cracked. I spin it off and drop it in the snow. I'm out of oxygen.

∽

The nearest hospital is in the village of Pheriche, a full day's hike from Base Camp.
— Scott Turner, *The High Alpinist's Survival Guide*

∽

9:51 PM, May 1
The Fixed Rope

It's overcast. And dark. The wind has died. Settling snow grazes my face. I'm gasping empty air, taking twenty breaths between each step. My black outer shell is frozen at my knees, elbows, and shoulders. My pain is gone. I'm out of sweat.

At the top of the last fixed rope, I swing you around, lower you feet first, and take your full weight with my harness. I shake with the strain, but feel no pain — a bad sign. I clip my jumar to the rope and sit for thirty breaths. Sleep would be bliss. I shake my head to stay awake. My hands feel warm, a symptom of hypothermia. I drink the last of my soup. It's now cold slush with refrozen chunks of tasteless meat. I suck out every last drop.

I stow my empty thermos, dig my heels into the snow, and lower you down. Numbers refuse to stay put and I lose count of my steps. I start over, get somewhere in the mid-twenties, then lose count again. I take another step.

About halfway down the fixed rope, my left crampon scrapes a rock and I slip. My right leg jackknifes. I don't fall, but end up crouching with my left leg extended. My heart rate crescendos. I hold the position until I recover. When I try to straighten, I find I can't. I'm too weak. I'm going to have to pull a tourist move. I close my eyes and lean back, trusting the fixed rope to support our combined weight. We sway on the rope but the ice screws hold. I take a lot more breaths, at least thirty. Slowly, I straighten my legs and resume our descent. I lose count three more times before we reach the end of the rope. I detach, move around so I can pull you, and trudge forward.

Ten or twelve steps farther and we come to a dark patch in the snow bypassed by the tourists' trail. My headlamp brushes a blue outer shell — Toilet Paper Woman. Her left knee is twisted to an ugly angle. Empty oxygen bottles litter the churned snow. My heart trips. The fall hadn't kill her, but she must be dead now.

A flash of gold on her left hand draws my attention. I slip out of my harness and brush away the snow to find a wedding ring. You always left yours at home. Her fingertips are black.

I cross her hands over her chest and clear the snow from her face. I pull back her oxygen mask. Her nose is black, too. So are the points of her cheeks. And the ridges above her eyebrows. I've never seen frostbite this bad. Way worse than what I had. She shouldn't have dug in with her feet. Blue Texan should have taught her how to self-arrest. Better yet, she should never have come to Everest in the first place.

I take off my mitts and gloves, touching her face with a bare finger. I can't feel a thing. "I don't," breath, "even know," breath, breath, "your real name."

Her response, when it comes, is faint. A whisper. I doubt I hear anything at all and wonder if it's an aural hallucination. But then it comes again, a slight rasp. "Wanda."

I remove her glacier glasses.

Her left eyelid flutters. "Like what you see?"

I gulp air. Snow swirls in my mouth.

Injured climbers are to be left where they fall. But you didn't leave Christine, just me. I only called Mom on the satphone because I couldn't remember if the Yukon rescue number was speed dial one or two. I guessed two. You'd programmed it as one.

My knee touches a spent oxygen bottle. I push it away, then stop and count the empties in the snow — one, two, three. Blue Texan said her entire team carried your book. "How many," breath, "oxygen bottles did you bring?" You wrote four was the preferred number for the Nepali route. I jam my gloves and mitts back on.

Wanda closes her eyes.

I roll her over. A fresh bottle juts from her pack. I connect it to her regulator and slide her mask over her face. "Breathe!"

New snow accumulates on Wanda's face. I brush it away. My vision starts to tunnel.

I unhook the bottle and attach it to my regulator. Fresh oxygen burns my throat. My flow rate is still set to maximum.

I dial it down. My head clears. Being alone on Logan was the worst night of my life. "I've got you, Wanda."

She doesn't respond.

I find Wanda's mitts and stuff her hands inside. Then I straighten her leg and slide her on top of you. When you're both on the sled, I lash her down. Camp IV isn't far, about two hundred metres at most. I slip on my harness and try to pull.

You won't even move a centimetre.

I try again.

Wanda's head lolls to the side.

I try one last time, throwing my weight against the rope.

Nothing.

It's obvious I don't have the strength to get you both down — I'll have to choose. Even with Mom making it very clear she'll never fund a second attempt or ever speak to me again, it's an easy choice. Atonement and revenge are inconsequential here. I attach the fresh oxygen to Wanda's regulator, untie her, and slide her from the sled. Gently. Then, I cut the rope and tip you into the snow.

Without oxygen, my head fuzzes and I wonder if I can still salvage everything. Maybe I could roll you off the mountain, like a cartoon snowball. Mom might accept that desecration. I tug on your shoulder.

You don't move.

I try dragging your feet.

Nothing.

Grab one foot.

Your boot comes off.

I lose my balance and slip to the snow.

Wanda coughs like a drowning kitten.

I shoot you the finger and go to her side. I up her flow rate. She settles.

I take back the oxygen and gulp down thick air. My head clears and I immediately see the flaws in cartoon physics. I abandon the snowball plan and secure Wanda to the sled, using all the rope.

I take out my satphone to warn Base Camp of the impending rescue. This time, I know which speed dial number it is. The handset doesn't power on. The casing is cracked in two places. I must have broken it when you pulled me off the Cornice Traverse. I pitch it into the snow. I'll have to ask either Blue Texan or Kiwi to make the call on their satphones. Right now, both leaders are probably in their tents, breathing fresh oxygen, making hot soup, and celebrating their clients' summits.

I slip into my harness again. Without your encumbrance, Wanda slides easily. After a few paces, I look back one final time. Mount Everest will continue to be your shrine. Tourists will continue to honour the great Scott Turner, author of *The High Alpinist's Survival Guide*. Climbers will continue to post photos. Journalists will continue to request interviews. Mom will continue to think I chose you over her. I read your book cover to cover that night on Logan, looking for any answer to explain what you did. I found nothing.

The irony of the whole thing is no real alpinist would ever let themselves be caught dead with a guidebook anywhere near a mountain. The Sherpas have certainly never read your book. I threw my copy into the Thames River my first week in Ontario. But both the animal crackers and the blue Americans all have theirs. And that realization means I might not have to leave you undesecrated after all. I reach into Wanda's pack and, sure enough, I find her copy. You even signed it. *Happy summiting, Scott Turner.*

Wanda's eyes flutter.

I give her the oxygen again. "Hold on."

She nods, or at least I think she does.

I place the book in your hands but it tumbles from your frozen fingers. I'll have to attach it, but with what? Wanda needs my rope. Christine has her scarf. Your clothing is too shredded. My vision begins to darken. My heart rate escalates. I loved you. Once. And then I get a vision of the solution, a clash of clichés my mother and every real alpinist is sure to understand — me kneeling, getting out my knife, stabbing down, cutting between your ribs, separating your frozen muscles with my fingers, and jamming *The High Alpinist's Survival Guide* deep into your chest, right where your heart was supposed to have been.

But I don't do it. Even if I had the strength to waste, it still wouldn't mean anything, because you'd never know. I return Wanda's book to her pack and take back the oxygen. We'll have to share it.